W9-BAF-945

d Eleven Vagabond Eleven Vagabond Eleven Vagabond

ALLAN CAMERON

ON THE HEROISM OF
MORTALS

Vagabond Voices
Glasgow

First published in June 2012 by
Vagabond Voices Publishing Ltd.,
Glasgow,
Scotland

ISBN 978-1-908251-08-4

Printed and bound in Poland

Cover design by Mark Mechan

Typeset by Park Productions

The publisher acknowledges subsidy towards this publication from Creative Scotland

For further information on Vagabond Voices, see the website,
www.vagabondvoices.co.uk

For Gianluca, Francesco,
Dominika and Barbara

Other works by the same author:

The Golden Menagerie (Luath Press, 2004)

The Berlusconi Bonus (Luath Press, 2005;
Vagabond Voices, 2010)

In Praise of the Garrulous (Vagabond Voices, 2008)

Presbyopia (Vagabond Voices, 2009)

Can the Gods Cry? (Vagabond Voices, 2011)

"Let us say that life is hard. Let us say it in a whisper,
'Life is hard.' Comrades, I implore you on behalf of millions
of people: Give us the right to whisper. You'll be so busy
constructing a new life that you'll never even hear us.
I guarantee it. We'll live out our entire lives in a whisper."

– Semyon Semyonovich in Nikolai Erdman's play,
The Suicide, which never got a chance to whisper its truth
until very shortly before the fall of the Soviet Union

"… true literature can exist only where it is created not by
diligent and trustworthy officials, but by madmen, hermits,
heretics, dreamers, rebels and sceptics. But when a writer
must be sensible and rigidly orthodox, when he must
make himself useful today, when he cannot lash out
at everyone like Swift or smile at everything like
Anatole France, there can be no bronze literature,
there can only be a paper literature, a newspaper literature,
which is read today and used for wrapping soap tomorrow."

– Yevgeny Zamyatin, "I Am Afraid"

"Among Soviet authors, Babel was one of the most committed
to the Revolution. He believed in progress, in everything getting
better. And they murdered this man."

– Ilya Ehrenburg speaking about Isaac Babel.

Contents

ON THE HEROISM OF
MORTALS

Only a Fool Can See

I am a fool and that brings its own benefits and satisfactions. There are, however, several dangers that may not be immediately obvious to more sensible persons. It's true, I saunter through life in an apparently directionless manner, but being almost invisible I have to keep my wits about me and, above all, my eyes open – otherwise those in pursuit of a title will collide with me constantly. They cannot see because they're concentrating on the greatness of their name. They are few, but around these parts they are increasing in number. They are nuclear physicists, company directors, judges, brain surgeons, politicians, head teachers, professors of medieval history, artists and writers. Dear me, I don't wish to suggest these are other than sublime *métiers*, but it is the doing of them and not the being them that is sublime.

The minute these practitioners clothe themselves in professional conformity, adopt the gravitas associated with their position and delight in all their badges of honour, they cease to be themselves and become less capable of performing their tasks.

These professionals will be considered the wisest of men as long as they do whatever everyone else in their profession is doing, but when they remember their independence of spirit, they are accused of immaturity, ingenuousness or even madness. Small wonder that they cling to the comfort of their titles and avoid the creative inspiration of their calling.

But what of the majority: those whose names were invented for oblivion, so that their acts could carry in the flow of history all the human good – the anonymous decency of those who put creativity before ambition. Surely we all remember the inventive teacher who inspired and in the staffroom only inspired contempt.

She sowed seeds in other minds that blossomed later, while she in early retirement struggled in part-time jobs and knew nothing of her ripened fruit.

Surely we recall the doctor who embarrassed the consultant with his correct diagnosis, and for showing not the absoluteness of his knowledge but its independent precision in the case in point. And that life-saving precision cost him his job. Another time, he will curb his exuberance and feign his ignorance so as not to reveal that of his superior.

Surely we know that those who write are stifled when they become writers and have to speak and sell themselves and run the business of being a writer – when they cease to be the silkworm and become the moth.

As they rush by (or bump into me after a moment's distraction on my part), they shout, "You're all words and no action." How right they are! I have nothing to do and a lot to say. I have no time to get the words out. They stumble over each other in their hurry to find a form and sequence on the page. Forgive, then, my erratic jottings, for what they lose in elegance they make up for in sincerity – always supposing that someone who has no certainties can be sincere.

This does not mean that I wish to write in a plain style – "pared-down" lines to satisfy the heart of every teacher of "creative writing", the ones who keep Orwell's diktats pinned to the office wall. Only the first one is valid because Orwell – great for what he wrote and did – would have made a lousy instructor in the art of letters. No, no, quite the opposite: I wish to play with the readers and string my sentences out – stretch the elasticity of their thoughts.

When I say I'm a fool, this is not urbane self-deprecation. Hell, no. Those who know me would laugh at your charity. How else to describe a man who does not know how to live, to love, to be loyal, to be courageous? But all knowledge starts with self-knowledge, and I know my limitations and I see the heroic greatness of others and the great hubris of others still. So let me tell you these stories based on things I have observed and things I have imagined. They are the most solid of my possessions, and willingly I share them with you. They lack structure, it's true, and they lack finery. Nor will I entice you with suspense or reassure you about the worthiness or relative worthiness of our society as some of our great writers do, especially when writing about a particular day of the week. There's nothing Panglossian about my stories. Nothing is in its place and nothing is the best possible. Everything is the product of the greatness of our neglected hearts and the weakness of our minds surfeited on mass-produced entertainments. No one is wholly good and no one wholly bad, for it is the moral greyness of our world that makes morality possible – and the lack of it.

To write a good book you need to lack certainty and discover style – or rather a style that suits your voice but is not your voice. To write a great book you *also* need humility, honesty and compassion. Even Nietzsche, who claimed to detest these things and counted "the overcoming of compassion among the *noble* virtues", was in fact overflowing with compassion – but like a schoolboy this embarrassed him. Compassion was girlish. And so his talent lent itself to ambiguity and occasionally to dangerous nonsense. That crippled compassion and his ecstatic style were his greatness. His flaw was that he often wrote extravagant absurdities and stooped to dangerous intellectual posturing – without however relinquishing his exquisite stylistic flourishes.

I am a little grey myself. I grew up in a grey, still industrial city, and somehow succeed in not belonging, even though I've never left Glasgow in my entire life. I've gone, it's true, for the odd weekend in the country. You know the kind of thing: an invite to some posh place with too many bedrooms, which have to be filled now and then. I may not be part of smart society, but I do get these summonses to observe, because they instinctively know that I can do that – observe, I mean. I stand in the corner and observe those who go in search of immortality. They think I will discover their greatness, but all I see is their sadness. We mortals enjoy life more because our nullification doesn't terrify us like it does them. They have all that stuff and it makes them feel more solid. That they are more ephemeral than their buildings and artworks seems to them an act of divine injustice, while to us it is merely divine mischief-making – a little fun at the expense of those who have no reason to complain.

But I have travelled far in my mind and have no great loyalty to my city – it is perfectly comfortable and its familiar architecture evokes in me little more than mild fondness. It has a kind soul, if a city can have a soul, but it also has a violent temper.

I went to its arts school, but dropped out because of a drug habit which took me another six years to conquer. Since then I have had a restless mind. I read and read. That barren activity fills my days, but what do I do with this accumulation of other people's wisdom? Very little really. I wander the Glasgow parks and engage people in conversation. This is not difficult in our city, and not just because of its famous talkativeness and banter. It seems that I'm not alone in my idleness. Well, idleness is what these blinded people like to call it. Idleness is not productive in their opinion, but what they cannot know is that idleness opens your eyes and makes you realise how much is going on: the intensity of emotions, the different tones of voice, the colour of our vain hopes, and the delight in each other's kindnesses. It is a world several light years away from the GROSS DOMESTIC PRODUCT, and it is entirely inhabited by heroes.

If I had been successful, I would have missed all this. Instead I would have travelled far and wide to visit identical hotels, and sunk into a bog of consumerist plenty. GDP would be my brother, and when the BBC announces an upward trend in growth or the Footsie One Hundred, my heart would leap with the same joy a man must feel on hearing he's a father. New life beckons and the cycle of nature is complete. They think that our universe is a delusion, but we think the same thing of theirs. Their madness is our wisdom. Of course. How could they think otherwise, given the extortionate price they had to pay at the entrance to that particular theme park – the dismal rides and games of that most dismal of pseudo-sciences.

I've only had one long-term sexual relationship in my life. It lasted three years and it was with a prostitute. I wasn't her pimp, you understand. I wasn't her pimp; I was her project, the beneficiary of her good, good heart. She saved me, but could not save herself. I left her only because of the violence of her life – all of it directed at her. I could never bear her heroism – her eternal baseless optimism. It started just days after I decided to come off drugs. She took me in like a lost puppy, and without her I would never have made it. Then I left her. Look, there were some scary fellas around those parts and she couldn't break free. I wasn't strong enough to help her. Not very heroic? No question of it. I am not a hero but an observer of heroism. You probably thought that I, being an ex-junkie and all that, am setting myself up as one of the heroic mortals. Not at all. I had a privileged childhood. My parents were working-class, and yet they gave me everything. My father worked on the railways, but he was a self-educated man and educated me.

He gave me enough to make me want more. I belong to the heroic mortals, but I am not one of them; that is why I am the right person to tell their tales. I don't want you to think this is all about class, although it does come into it. Ultimately, even those who sell their souls and close their eyes are all forced to be a little heroic. Only fools like me can mix candour with cowardliness.

The French would call me *déclassé*: neither fish nor fowl. Certainly I have never really worked. I was and am a spoilt child. This has to be the starting point for anyone who wants to understand me. Many a middle-class child would have envied me. Like everything else, privilege takes many forms and mine was amongst the best. The only child of a loving and hardworking couple, I lacked nothing and wanted everything. Want nearly destroyed me and when I woke from my surfeit of pleasures I suddenly found that the delicacies offered by consumer society even in the sixties no longer attracted me. Only leisure had any hold. My only desire was never to be hurried. I occupy my mind, but only in ways that I find genial in any given moment.

I have of course played at various things. I have written reviews for *The Weegie-Board*, an alternative literary magazine set up in the early seventies. Once very radical, it now sounds like an elderly headmaster handing out cliché'd compliments to his favourite pupils. The corporation gives it a few quid every year and it employs three people, two of whom are children of its original founders once hell-bent on the destruction of property and all privilege, and the third is a smart young man with literary pretensions who also happens to be the boyfriend of the leader of the Labour group on the council. They still give me the odd review and I enjoy the status of venerable layabout.

Of course you'll think that a person like me will never have the self-discipline to finish a collection of short stories such as this one. I see your point and in part share your low opinion of myself. But I should point out that it takes great discipline to disdain all the pleasures of this bounteous post-industrial heaven, to reject the crashing din of lies emitted by our mass media and not to fall for the next crackpot conspiracy theory that happens by with siren call – just for the hell of it, just to believe in something and savour its small relief. Perhaps there is after all some small measure of courage in my cowardly existence.

My real contempt is for the immortal gods – the true aristocrats of our universe. They run no risks and cannot know the meaning of tragedy. They look at our faulted, gruelling and unsteady existences, and envy us, but still don't understand. For them all emotions are muted: the worst that can happen to them is a slight disappointment, which in any case will shrink to the minuscule, as eternity pounds along its endless journey, and the best that can happen is some faint excitement probably ruined by the disdainful laughter of their fellow-gods, languid and worldly-wise after millennia of existence.

But then, don't our rich – so powerful and celebrated – also act a little like the gods? Languid and worldly-wise they affect a nonchalance that is not theirs. That too is heroism of a kind.

I know a writer and knew him when he used to write the most splendid prose I've ever read. Now he's just a writer, which means he's always on television or the radio. He writes about everything as if he understands it all. Last week he wrote an article about the humble and often maligned tampon which, according to him, changed Western society and next week he will prove beyond all reasonable doubt that texting, contrary to popular opinion, will improve our children's spelling. There is no limit to the powers of his intrepid intellect.

I did some research for him on his best book, by which I mean the one critics liked and were right to do so. Another won the Booker and made him rich. Then he became a writer and spent all his time trying to recreate those moments of exhilaration – success with the critics and then with the public. But his writing has no freshness now, and I used to feel sorry for him until one day he came jogging by. I was seated and unusually had removed my cap, because of the heat. It lay upturned on the bench beside me, on top of some papers and the book I was reading. He looked at me quizzically as though half remembering something but unsure that he wanted to. He didn't see me because he was in too much of a hurry to be even more famous. He didn't recognise me because he wouldn't have been able to recognise his old self. Success and, more particularly, wealth divide us from our past and those who inhabited it. He saw me as a beggar, a profession I would never engage in: too much like hard work. As he passed he dropped a pound coin in my cap, where it sat lonely but important and cushioned by the silky, padded lining and the manufacturer's coat of arms, a little greasy from my hair. I keep it still, that coin only remarkable for the manner in which I acquired it, that round unit by which we measure the ultimate worth of our increasingly brittle bones held together by our sweating flesh – and keep it well polished on my desk as a symbol of the folly of the wise.

The Hat

How many times did my grandfather tell me the story? So many, and every time there were new details; some of them conflicted with others very slightly. Perhaps he wanted to soften the cruelty of the situation; undoubtedly he told me more as I grew older. I think I know what happened; it was a moment he clung to and that shines through those terrible years. But I listened; of his grandchildren I was the one who listened without showing any impatience at what we all knew by heart. It was a story that gained its sacredness in the retelling. It was a holy story that spoke of man's humanity to man.

My grandfather was born Tadeusz Szlos, a Polish Jew from Vilnius. In early 1943, he had been on the run for months and had reached as far south as Romania. He wanted to get to Hungary, which at the time appeared to be the safest place for a Jew to be, in the Nazi Empire and its satellites. Unknown to him, the Siege of Stalingrad was entering its final stages, and for him all seemed hopeless. Life was about survival for the next few days. He dared not consider a definitive solution, an escape from persecution across a border now too distant even for a resourceful man like him. He thought only about his next meal, a place to sleep and rest, and a slow, circuitous movement towards a country that could only be considered less unfriendly than the others.

Having slept in the woods for several nights with a small bag of provisions now entirely used up, he went down a gentle slope towards a small rural township. He would never remember the name, although he studied a map of the area on several occasions. "I sometimes wonder," he once said, "about the existence of that nameless place, and yet it was there that the most extraordinary thing occurred. So small it was. A gesture of the hand that consumed not even a second of time and a movement of half a metre. Without it I would not be here and nor would you."

Always that. Always harping on about our insubstantiality, the wonder of his continued existence and, by inheritance, my own. Always about the story of the hat and not, for instance, the nuns near Prague who hid him in a coal cellar until the end of the war. Always because of the smallness of the act, its quickness and its anonymity. He would hold the hat on his knees and shake his head in disbelief. Even as he lay dying of a final angina attack, I suspect he still felt the strangeness of that moment in which the rim of the hat slipped over his hair and, being slightly too large, sat gently on his ears pushing them outwards. That a life's continuance could hang on so slight a thing seemed to madden and reassure him at the same time.

The difficulty in remembering the town was indeed its own anonymity, its unexceptional presence in that unchanging landscape. The church, the central square, the plain but solid architecture, the drabness of its citizens, now weighed down by the thing they detested most, the unpredictability of war. He moved amongst them quickly, studying their faces carefully as he went. Survival meant staying in the town for the shortest possible time, and discovering who could help. A man on the run is like a beggar; he learns to read a person's face, to know who might be compassionate enough to assist if the risk is not too high. A buxom woman with a kindly smile and a little sadness around the eyes was surely a reliable choice. He sidled up with a now well-practised artfulness, a mixture of assertiveness and supplication. Those who survived a month on the run had a good chance of surviving much longer, he would say, only luck could get you through that first month.

"Madam, could I have a word," he said in his heavily accented Romanian, but she answered him in German, a language he knew very well. "Yid! Filthy Yid! You're the people who brought this evil war upon us." The idiocy of her words only just touched him, while a few years earlier he would have been outraged by such bigotry. His principal thought was that he had misjudged, and now had to escape. She continued, as though addressing eve-ryone around, but they ignored her and continued about their business: "My son volunteered and now he's dead on the Eastern Front." Fortunately she now appeared to forget my grandfather as she poured out her grief at her son's early death. He slipped into a side street and headed towards the church. There were plenty of German and Romanian soldiers around in the border area of Bukovina, where two allies met and the principal language of the people was Ukrainian. A funeral procession appeared and he pushed himself in amongst the mourners. No one appeared to mind or question his presence. Bareheaded, he allowed himself to be drawn along by a crowd of black-suited men all wearing hats, mostly of a similar kind to the one he would hold on his knee as he told this story. It was a homburg, a cheap woollen one but neat in the stitch work attaching the inner leather band around the rim. It was a very dark brown, and shiny with use.

My grandfather was calm again. He had learned to rapidly regain clear-headedness. Like a hunted animal, his senses could pick up the slightest change in circumstance, which he then swiftly assessed. But what happened next had no slightness about it. When it came, it brought not agitation, but a numbness, a terror, a feeling of complete impotence. An open personnel carrier lurched into the street and German soldiers ran off in all direc-tions. Others halted the procession and only let it continue even more slowly than before, as they randomly selected mourners to show their papers. My grandfather didn't have any.

He looked around and it was immediately clear that there was no escape. Surely he would be selected. Just as he let that sense of resignation seep into his consciousness like a cold steel blade, he felt the hat's rim on his hair. Before the war, that unexpected act would have given him a jump and instinctively he would have turned to see who was responsible, but with his heightened senses he did not react and immediately felt reassured. He was not alone. Someone had come unbidden to his rescue.

My grandfather judged the distance to the German roadblock and then waited as they shuffled slowly forwards until he had covered half of it. Then he turned to see the hatless man who was his benefactor. He saw an elderly man, smartly dressed for the times. The man had a moustache and goatee beard. Both very grey of course. He looked respectable and slightly severe, a teacher perhaps or even a judge. My grandfather tried to catch his attention, vainly wishing to express his gratitude, but the stiff-backed man refused to allow their eyes to meet. There was no quiver of a smile or acknowledgement of what had passed between them. So convincing was his expressionless face that my grandfather looked around in search of another hatless head, but there were none to be seen. He would never again see that face, "but I would recognise him like a brother if I ever saw him," he would say with a determination that suggested such a thing could still happen – that he wanted to search the world for a face that could no longer have existed by the time he told me the story.

Just before my grandfather could reach the soldiers, his benefactor was called out because of his conspicuous hatlessness. They demanded his papers, which he produced with deliberate slowness for a vigorous man, and they grudgingly returned them. By then my grandfather was passing between the soldiers, somehow certain that he was going to be safe. Once he was, he turned only to see the back of the man hurrying up a hill away from the funeral with a sprightly step. His back was turned, and this enigmatic soul disappeared forever. A moment later, my grandfather's mind returned to the business of keeping alive, but he was always to keep that hat.

When I was a young child, he would still wear it, but it was becoming very worn, and in his last years he kept it on his desk, on a stand he had specially made. I was seventeen at the time of his death in 1990. As a teenager, I liked to go into his study to chat to him. He was an educated man and a polyglot. He could talk on any subject, often with passion. His ideas reflected his generation: he became a member of the Communist Party once he got to Britain, and he left at the time Hungary was invaded. But he remained a communist for the rest of his life; the Labour Party, of which he was a fully paid-up member until he died at the age

ALLAN CAMERON

of eighty-two, never satisfied his radical belief in humanity. "Too English," he would say, which expressed his mixture of admiration and contempt for the nation that had provided him with asylum but often seemed to have done so less out of humanist generosity than out of patrician grandness that cannot distinguish between those who do not belong to its class. And he had been useful with his knowledge of nuclear physics, although his politics did stunt his career.

He was a man without animosity – a detachment that he learned perhaps from his fearful years on the run. "I was lucky," he would say, "I never saw the inside of a camp." However much the conversation ranged from language to literature, from science to religion and from politics to peace, it always came back to that hat that sat on the table, a symbol of the past, of brutal times and the human goodness that had somehow prevailed. He did not just retell the story. He spoke of the man, who he might have been and what he might have done after the war. Where had he gone in that most fluid part of Europe, where everyone was fleeing from one side to the other, often with a moment's notice? Should he have sought him out? I felt that what tormented him was not so much the fact that he had never been able to thank the man as his desire to find out what kind of man might have made such a gesture. "Any kind of man," I would say, "surely any man – or woman – is capable of such an act." But he did not look convinced by my answer. Perhaps he felt that he was going to die without knowing an essential clue to human nature.

Later still, he started to obsess about the hat itself. "Have you seen that?" he once said. "The hat was made in Vienna. This was a much-travelled man, someone with a cosmopolitan background. An intellectual, no doubt."

"You just want him to be someone like yourself," I countered, "to reassure you that his decency was of your own kind."

He took this criticism seriously, and looked at me with genuine admiration.

"He could easily have been a local squire, who on a single trip to Vienna, the capital before the First World War, took advantage of the opportunity to buy a hat, albeit a hat that you have already defined as cheap," I expanded on the argument.

"You're right," he muttered as though bending before an unpalatable truth. "He might have been a local, small-town judge, a devout Catholic and full of those minor prejudices so typical of a man of such a station in those times. And yet he could sense the injustice of my plight and took swift action. All it cost him was a cheap hat and a few moments of bother with the German soldiers."

"Maybe, but he alone amongst all those people took action. The others resisted passively; he resisted actively. There's a huge difference."

"Only those who were in a radius of a few feet of me could have taken that action. Some of those might also have had no papers or papers that were in some way defective. Those were the times. The difference between him and the others might not have been so great." And of course he was right. That was the joy of keeping his company: he could pick over the tiny details of life, and that momentary act of generosity fascinated him primarily because of its anonymity.

"He might have been a bank manager or even an elderly clerk, passed over for promotion precisely because of his intellectual interests," my grandfather continued to speculate.

"There you go again," I argued, "always letting your imagination run away and in a single direction. You are certain that he suffered in some way. Perhaps only in a small way. You think that only someone who has suffered can show compassion, but how can you be sure?"

"I can't of course," he answered darkly, "but statistically it is more probable. When you're older, you'll understand."

I hated that argument then; I probably use it now.

"He was not that conventional. This hat has a hard rim," I pointed out, "and yet he removed it with two fingers and a thumb around the start of the dent running along the top."

"My God, you're right," he said with a wry but friendly smile. "It is even more worn and shiny in those three spots, pressing under the crease and spoiling the hat's perfect symmetry. And I always used the brim."

"I know, and I expect most Europeans did. Isn't there something slightly American about that way of putting a hat on one's head and removing it? Cinematic perhaps?"

"You're quite a girl," he beamed, and I remember those words so well. "You should be a detective." Then in a faintly troubled tone, he continued, "This only adds to the uncertainty around this enigmatic figure." His smile returned immediately; this was his favourite subject.

A week or so after that conversation, he summoned me to his study, which was unusual. He sat down gravely and signalled me to do the same. It was almost like an interview, and certainly quite unlike our customary behaviour. He looked at the ceiling as though he had a clearly defined thought very difficult to put into words even in his head. He then sat up straight to glance at his papers, which turned out to have nothing to do with what he wanted to say, and finally coughed gently. "I wanted to speak to you about something of great importance. I have been thinking for several months about who should be the person to whom I shall leave my most treasured possession." By then, I knew exactly where he was going, and was feeling a little disappointed. My grandfather owned many beautiful things: books, paintings and various objects collected on his travels to academic conferences. "It will probably come as something of a surprise, but I know you will be delighted that I have chosen you and not one of the other grandchildren. They will want things of value; they're all a little bourgeois, you know." I nodded guiltily. "You are ... and I feel a little silly telling you this ... my favourite grandchild by far. I suppose because I see a lot of myself in you. That's how it is. Crass, I know. But it comes down to that. I know that by leaving you the hat that saved my life I am declaring my preference, and that might please your mother, but it won't my other children ... and their offspring." I forgot in that moment my lapse into acquisitiveness and began to feel embarrassment at being crowned with that anonymous hat. A feeling of great pleasure and great awkwardness. What do you say when chosen for such a personal gift? It was as if he had offered to leave me part of his soul.

After he died, there was another strange event – a kind of informal ceremony – at which my mother and my aunts and uncles handed over the precious hat with its stand. "It's a man's hat," my mother's brother stated the obvious. "In a delicate state," my mother added. They were not discourteous, but much was left unsaid. I was in no doubt that they found my grandfather's decision quite bewildering; they perhaps had not noticed our closeness. As often happens in families, no one observes what's going on under their noses. Family relationships are often based on the intimacy of mutual incomprehension. My mother's eldest brother was the most generous – in the manner of older siblings – and never lost an opportunity for judicious advice. "My father has paid you a great honour," he said as he placed a patriarchal arm around my shoulder while leaving the other hand free to wave a finger authoritatively, "one that might quite reasonably have been due to me. But my father was a very good judge of character, and if he chose you, he did so for a good reason. You must show yourself worthy of the trust he has placed in you."

So the hat was moved from his desk to my bedroom and then to the various studies that I have had in various homes. I have not been in the habit of speaking about it to many people, but it is the thing that holds me to my grandfather, to whom I was closer than to my own parents – with their perennial squabbling, their competitiveness between themselves and jointly with others, and their great love of possessions. For strangely, when that hat became part of me, I lost all my hankering for other things. With it I also inherited from my grandfather's very limited needs – excepting the greedy and insatiable need to understand, which is of course no small thing and requires the right kind of job and the right kind of mind.

I have failed in life. Of course. We all do.

I have failed as an academic. I have failed to formulate my ideas and pass them on to others. I have failed to engage with colleagues, so fixated was I with my own research. I rejected all those compromises you have to make if you're to get anywhere, but compromised with those outside work who made demands upon my time. Somehow I have betrayed my talents, when that was the thing I least wanted to do. How is it that my grandfather got all these things right, even after those years of suffering? He thought that I was like him; how wrong he was.

I have failed as a wife, thank God. I was critical of my parents' shallow marriage, and wanted something much better for myself. I was the first to marry a non-Jew, although my parents were both atheists, as was my grandfather. Oddly my parents – particularly my mother – were against my marrying outside – outside what exactly? The race? That's nonsense. They would, it appears, have preferred me to marry a practising Jew, in spite of their contempt for such people. And yet I cannot deny that they had their part of the truth, however absurd it might seem. When I look at my husband, my "English" husband ... but how can I say that? What am I, if not English? When I look at my English husband, I feel this instinctive irritation at the magnitude of his complacency. He is not a bad man – not a particularly good one either, I now think. He's not uneducated – a qualified GP – but he shares that anti-intellectualism of the English middle classes. He wants nothing that disturbs his views, his certainties, and the pleasantness of his life. His beer, his football matches, his car, his climbing, his son perhaps, and oh, his wife. Once he found me an asset: good-looking, sharp, well educated, he thought. Definitely an asset. But the world has changed and now he finds me a little extravagant – and not so pretty as I was. He calls me selfish, because I follow my career, and now that assertion has no effect on me whatsoever. It is not the emptiness of my marriage that worries me; it is my lack of belief in ever finding a man worthy of my love. I think that I want someone like my grandfather, who I thought a not uncommon type. I want a man who is passionate about ideas but calm about his needs and his relationships, exactly as my grandfather was. But do such men grow in this land of cloistered consumerism? Do they only grow from the more acidic earth into which blood has been spilt in vast quantities? What can we expect of a country that hasn't known the misery of warfare since the English Revolution briefly turned it on its head? My husband comes home and talks brightly of nothing, and when I stare at him with disenchantment clearly stated in my eyes, he accuses me of being moody and neurotic. Those words! If only he knew what a compliment they are; so much better than the other ones he showers on me all sugared with condescension. I know that I will leave him once my son has finished his studies. Not long now he is eighteen years of age.

I have failed as a parent. God forgive my soul! I had such hopes for him. I wanted him to be called Thaddeus, but my husband insisted on Geoffrey. *Nomen omen.* I do not know him now, and that is why I write. I came home last night and Geoffrey was in his room with a girl. I heard them laughing as I climbed the stairs, and was going to leave them alone, but he called out to me, "Mum, come in here. You're going to love this." Of course, the statement contained an obvious menace, but parenthood involves these things now. I was expecting a humiliation. Still I knocked on the door. I was actually expecting a teenage display of inappropriate sexual behaviour – inappropriate for other people's eyes, that is. "Come in, come in, Mum! Nothing naughty going on here, is there Jill? Well, not yet anyway." Jill produced a roar of unrestrained laughter that contained only a hint of unease when at last I stood in the doorway. She must have noticed my expression of horror, but she could not have understood the reason.

Though slightly drunk, Geoffrey knew immediately that he had gone too far. He adopted a defensive attitude that I knew was going to be stubborn. Jill's laughter slowly died down. "What do you think you're doing?" I sneered coldly, snarled perhaps. Something broke within me. He pretended not to understand, "Just having a little fun with Jill. Nothing serious, you know. Just a little fun."

"Jill can go to hell, for all I care," I said.

"I'll not put up with this," he said grandly and as he stood up unsteadily, he extended his hand to Jill to help her do the same.

They approached me together, Jill clinging to her brave cavalier. I ignored her and extended my hand in front of me to stop his chest. He felt the hardness of my hand; he felt my anger. "What have you done to my grandfather's hat?"

"She's mad," Jill said.

The heavily ribbed hatband was gone altogether, revealing brown wool cloth of a slightly lighter brown. The crease was covered with stickers and, worst of all the other indignities suffered by my grandfather's hat, my son had taken an orange felt-tip pen and inflicted on it a few words that would be enough to change things between us forever, "Running away from the Nazis". Was this all he had taken from the story? The courage it took to survive Nazism was lost on him and was no part of his life. For him that period was history, and history is the past with which we have no emotional connection.

"What the hell does that mean?" I asked.

Geoffrey giggled at the absurdity of it all. "I was telling Jill how we all descend from a hat. That's right, Mum? A hat."

I was now suspended between anger and exhaustion. Unfortunately I was unable to release the anger. That might have saved our relationship. I was lost for words, and there seemed to be no fixed point on which I could start to explain the sacrilege of his act and how important that mean little object was. It was made of wool, cardboard, leather and grosgrain ribbon, but it was a world of ideas that has been lost, of sacrifices made, of loves ignored for the greater good, of suffering and of hopelessness. And out of that my grandfather had created his life anew in a foreign land and given it all he had.

"Clearly your generation doesn't have the imagination to empathise with the suffering of others." I knew, as soon as I said it, that "your generation" was an unfortunate choice of words – for me, that is; they put me in a weak position. I've always known that when speaking to the younger generation you must never moralise. I've managed this with my own students, but with my son it was next to impossible.

I stared at him – I must have glowered.

He coolly enjoyed the silence, and at one stage he briefly ceased to return my stare in order to share a knowing smile with his girlfriend. He then waited in relaxed silence for a moment of his own choosing. If we've given our children anything, it's self-confidence. They have it in such abundance, they hardly know it.

It's possible that what I took for self-confidence was actually his ability to hide his weakness behind a knowing exterior – bravado, also known as dramatic effect. We do forget what it's like to be young. At what seemed precisely the right moment, he started to speak in a world-weary drawl, as an overworked employer might with a recalcitrant employee. "Look, Mum, we'd had a hard day and we needed to let off a bit of steam. Exams are coming up and we're under pressure, you know. I suppose it's difficult for you to remember. I'm sorry if I've upset you." Jill looked up at him, admiring of his magnanimity. "It's a hat, Mum. People are more important than things," said the young man who had campaigned remorselessly for us to buy him a 4x4. "Your grandfather, I'm sure, was much more than a hat – a cheap one at that."

I knew that I too had to dissemble – to hide my anger and hurt. "That's okay. It is, as you say, just a hat, a cheap hat now too delicate to wear. But it was the only thing my grandfather left me, and it was, for him, the most important."

He had his chance. He and Jill could have walked past me while wishing me good night, and then gone off to the pub to discuss the whole affair with renewed hilarity. That would have been the proper hedonistic thing to do, but Geoffrey also wanted to win the argument – which argument he was not quite sure, but he wanted to win it anyway. "Have you ever asked yourself," he spoke deliberately, as though it were his onerous duty to reveal to me what everyone else would have found obvious, "why your grandfather only left you an old hat. I'm sure he softened the blow with all kinds of explanations. Auntie Sarah got a Toni del Renzio."

"You know who Toni del Renzio was, do you?" I was speaking contemptuously to my own son. We let these things happen to us without realising that the way back may be very difficult.

"No, and I don't care. Better than an old hat."

"So value is purely monetary, even if you don't know why an

object has value. It's simply enough that the market gives it value
– that the general consensus does."

"That's about it. You've got it in one, Mum. Well done!"

"Even if, as was the case, the artist in question doesn't give a
damn about any of that shit?"

"Right again. And I'd be much more envious if it had been a
Salvador Dali."

"Who everyone has heard of. So that is it? That's all it is."

"Listen, Mum, I've got just two things to say here: you're a snob,
and obsessed with values – European values – that are dead. And
secondly, I don't care about art. It makes no sense. The surrealists,
for Christ's sake!"

"So why do you care if one of Sarah's children is going to inherit
such a painting?" I asked.

"Because it's worth money," he seemed angry at my obtuseness,
and Jill failed to suppress a giggle.

"I think you should know that my grandfather was the person
dearest to me in my life," I said and purposefully refrained from
saying "your great-grandfather".

"Really? You know, Mum, you just live in the past. Dad and I
are alive: what about us?"

"Better to live in the past than only in the present, because you
can't understand the present without understanding the past."

"That's a cliché, Mum."

"That's what I hate about you, Geoffrey, you make me talk in
clichés."

"Nice! A mother telling her son she hates him."

"I didn't say I hate you. I said one thing about you I hate. Aren't
we all a bit like that? It's clear from this conversation that there
are things about me that you find contemptible, to say the least."

"Not contemptible, Mrs Henderson, not contemptible. We just
don't quite understand why you're so upset," Jill unwisely butted in.
Her intention was to smooth things over and bring the conversation to an end, but she alienated both of us. She didn't know that I
preferred to be addressed as Professor Szlos. He looked at her darkly
to intimate that her silence would be preferred. Family business.

"Right again, Mum, I do find things contemptible about you. You're not part of our world or even our family. Dad and I do things together. We laugh at you, you know, and your obsessions – your quaint politics, 'save the whale' crap and that stupid hat. Get a life, Mum."

"Loosen up!" Jill hazarded, still unaware of the risks involved.

"I have a life," I said. "A very good life, thank you very much," although that last statement did require a little bravado on my part. Each generation carried its mask. I felt in that moment that my life had been a series of wasted energies, but to have revealed that would have lost me the argument. "You can have political beliefs and still have a sense of humour, you know. You can care about humanity as a whole, and still care about that restricted humanity that is your friends and relations. In fact, one without the other makes no sense. And friends and family are all you're left with, really, because we can change so little beyond that."

"How sad for you that you're left with us."

"You know that's not what I meant. Family and friends are the most important thing, but they will not benefit if you and they don't engage with the world beyond. That was the essential idea that your great-grandfather carried across the channel – he and many others. They were fleeing oppression and not looking for utopia, just for safety, and they had learned many things. He passed them on to me, and I have held them dear. If I haven't passed them on to you, then I, most probably, am at fault."

He winced at that one, and so did I, because I'd used one of the basest parental tricks, but a very effective one. They left after that, muttering a few slightly conciliatory remarks I cannot remember. He was unhappy with the conversation, because he had not achieved what he wanted. He hadn't flattened me. He hadn't made me cry or supplicate like a desperate mother. He found me cold perhaps – too rational. We all have our own natures, I suppose, and the manner of his leaving sealed the rift for me. When the door closed, I realised that the son I had loved was no longer the son I had loved. I had always been aware of our differences, of course, but now I felt that I didn't know him and, worse and more strangely, I felt that I didn't want to know him – the pursuit of that ideal would only lead to a further deterioration in our relationship. Perhaps a detachment of this kind is inevitable when children grow up – to a greater or lesser extent – but in our case, the rupture was dramatic and irreversible.

Geoffrey is not entirely in the wrong, of course. Perhaps I am aloof, and aloofness triggers a desire to rebel. He wanted to shock me out of it. I see that now, and that's not an entirely mistaken desire in a young man, but it has to be accompanied by something else – a worldview that isn't entirely based on personal satisfaction. It made me think about those post-war years when, for so long, it appeared that society would simply continue to progress in an unbroken line. Increasing affluence passes through two stages: first it liberates people from the drudgery of survival and they are even freer to think beyond themselves and open up their minds to new ideas; second it becomes an end in itself, making people feel self-important – surely such wealth means superiority – and closes off their minds to new ideas and challenges. My generation, which straddles those two stages, is responsible for the degradation of our values. We started by attacking our parents not without reason, but we did so with arrogance and self-righteousness. We should at least have held to the values we proclaimed so loudly, or at least, we shouldn't have reneged on them no sooner had we reached the age in which the reins of power were passed our way. Small wonder then that our children were born cynics; they only had to observe the inconsistencies of their parents.

Generations are different countries, but they cohabit the same physical space – dividing almost every household. They may speak the same language – or almost – but the philosophical parameters through which they filter that language are different. Moreover the distinctions are gradated, because generations are gradated, and this gradation is exacerbated by people who are brought up by very young or very old parents or, like myself, are primarily influenced by grandparents. Of course the distinctions between countries are not discrete either. Intermarriage, migration and shifting borders mean that countries are never eternal entities. But generations are like countries in that the cultural difference is about the same: some continuity and some discontinuity. In this chaos, it is only possible to discern trends over fairly long periods – decades at least.

There is currently a stench of the thirties. It is not only the financial crisis, because miserably more than a whiff of chauvinism and xenophobia predated it. But the financial crisis will undoubtedly make things worse. My son Geoffrey will not be able to avoid political choices forever, and which way he will go is unfortunately beyond my comprehension. What is clear is that whatever influences may bear down on him, they will not come from this home or from our family history. He is lost to me, but I cannot wholly despair of him.

As history repeats itself, some will go to the right and some will go to the left. Many lessons will have to be learnt from scratch. That is a tragedy, but it is one we should expect if we take a glance at history. Yet I believe – no, I should say that I hope – that this new generation will eventually discover an internationalism, an intellectual openness and, above all, a compassionate humanity even more evolved than the ones my grandfather brought over here with his hat. That would be progress, if progress there be.

He – Or Is It Him?

"Maybe," he said, his eyes wide open with the provocation that negates.

He carved the still bleeding joint with skill, fulfilled his only domestic chore to signify his station in the house – the holder of all keys, all levers of power, all needs, all judgements, all hopes, all discernments of the past. He placed a slice – wafer thin, its lightness surely expressing the sharpness of his brain – also on her plate. The gesture – so munificent it too contained no weight – found universal delight amongst the generous profusion engendered by his loins, which he'd arranged around the table in the manner he saw fit. And then he sat down as can only sit one who sits snugly within himself, comfortably within his skin.

"No, absolutely not," she replied. "I am the product of a single-parent family myself."

"That may well be," he laughed gently as a person might, if privy to the actual way humankind was wrought. "That's not my point, and if I can be so bold, that's statistically irrelevant. A family, you see, should ideally be made up of the following elements: a father," he smiled graciously, "a mother," he pointed to a woman with his knife after momentarily forgetting where he'd placed her in the scheme of things, "and the children of course," he waved his inclusive hand to express all he had achieved, those silent witnesses to his paternal gifts.

"I don't care if I'm the only happy child of a single-parent family in the world. My case alone can prove that a child may even gain by such a situation. I do not miss my father or a father figure. I am complete, and you cannot convince me of a deprivation I have never felt."

"Of course, my dear," he said through gritted teeth, "you cannot appreciate what you've never had."

"Nor can you," it was her turn to laugh, "appreciate the closeness of my mother's love that opened every door to a meaningful adult life, and kept those shut that lead to greed and disdain."

He considered her words with evident distaste. It was not just the content of what she said; it was also her methodology. He was accustomed to bludgeoning people with statistics, but she was defending herself with her exceptionalism. The powerless are more numerous, but inexplicably statistics always prefer the powerful, and provide every justification for their decisions after they have made them. She didn't seem to care. She exuded too much self-confidence for a woman – there was surely something unnatural in that. The only specificity he found interesting was his own, and he was sure that everyone else shared that passion – for his, not theirs, of course. Outside his own specificity, he felt that the "general good" should reign, and happily the general good always coincided with what was good for the English middle classes.

Initially uncertain about his strategy for parrying her argument, he resorted to what he knew to be a platitude – dangerous with her but it bought him time. "We English," he said, "are a traditional people because we know the value of holding on to what has been tried and tested in the past. I'm sure your mother would agree."

She looked at him in surprise, and he finally caught the argument that had eluded him – a good statistical one. "Look, you may well have had an acceptable childhood," he expounded confidently and smilingly, "and even a good education – you seem an articulate girl – but the fact is that the slightest shift in the success parameters of a child's early life can produce *huge* differences in outcomes in terms of happiness and competence. Did you know, for instance, that if you're born in August, your life chances are far lower than if you're born in September?"

"Statistically," she commented, "but there will be successful people born in August and failures in September."

"So," he ignored her point, "how much greater must be the disadvantage if a child grows up without a father."

"But what kind of father?"

"If you'll just let me finish my argument," he looked at her fiercely and his wife seemed terrified by the direction the conversation was taking; "the point I'm making is also a practical one, you see. If you're born in August, you're always the youngest, weakest and least mature of your class. Equally if the family doesn't have a car..."

"My mother's Swedish."

He looked stunned and for a few seconds all the words he had constructed in his head melted into a haze, and at the same time he struggled to give form to her words. "You mean your mother had a Swedish car?" he concluded, evidently impressed.

"No, I said that my mother is Swedish."

"What has that got to do with anything?"

"You said what we English think – by which you mean a statistical English person, but I doubt that even the majority of English men think like you. You said my mother would probably agree with you. But she wouldn't and anyway she's Swedish."

"But I said that ages ago, and now you've interrupted my train of thought."

"Yes, I was waiting for you to finish, which took patience, as you do ramble on a bit. When you got to the part about the car, I had to interrupt, I'm sorry."

"But I haven't finished my point."

"But you have. I'm not saying that in this unequal society, various factors don't influence the outcomes in children's lives, but they don't determine them absolutely. We also make our own lives, and my mother made a family life in which I lacked absolutely nothing. Now that's an absolute for you."

"Absolutely nothing?" he jeered. "I would have thought you lacked something many would consider to be of great consequence: a father."

"Yes, I lacked that, I suppose. And he might have added to my life – but he might just as easily have been a violent drunk."

"Do we know where your father came from, given how invisible he has become?" he abandoned all pretence of the gracious gentleman.

"Yes we do. He was Irish."

He smiled exultantly as though to say now everything had been explained.

"I say 'was' because we know nothing about what happened to him. Apparently he left when I was six months old."

"Your mother couldn't keep him, then?"

She laughed contemptuously, "My mother would never have wanted *to keep* anyone. It was not just that intellectually she abhorred the concept of possession; it simply wasn't in her nature."

"But clearly he didn't want to stay."

"Clearly. My mother loved him, she says, but he needed her resources, which were probably being diverted in my direction. He was an unemployed artist. He had ambitions. It's an old story – but they parted amicably. She would have liked to have heard from him now and then. Maybe something happened to him. Our lives are not solid things, you know; it must be difficult for a man in your position to know that."

Once again the normally loquacious man appeared to have used up his stock of words. He studied her, and considered briefly the fluidity of relationships in the modern world. He failed to formulate a precise vision of it: he was English, middle-class, male, wealthy, surrounded by a subservient family, and part of a network that went back to childhood and a school tie with narrow strips of red and white alternating with a thick band of blue on which a silver canon was embossed at regular intervals. Who could be more solid than that?

"I understand," he said finally, "that I may have expressed myself badly. Of course there can be exceptions – although not many, if you want my opinion. You, on the other hand, must learn not to take things so personally and not to perceive offence where none was intended."

"No, you didn't express yourself badly." This time, she was the one who smiled with a slight air of superiority, or was it impatience?

"You have, in fact, made yourself very clear. You feel that my people are inferior to your people, and that your ways of doing things are the only ones to be prized. I could not disagree more. You, no doubt, pity us and feel that we're unable to discern the deficiencies in our lives. But you see I feel exactly the same way about your lifestyle: how are your children going to be influenced by their upbringing? Here is your family," she copied his gesture when he introduced them to her, "and they revolve around you like small planets orbit the sun. One planet is slightly bigger and that one represents your silent wife."

The silent wife was silent no longer. She sprang from her chair with a leap so unexpected that everyone else jumped in theirs. "How dare you!" she cried. "How can you come into our house as a guest and insult us? It isn't always those who speak up most who think the most – and feel. You two speak of things that concern us as though we weren't here." And then the mother lunged at her across the table, only just failing to grab the younger woman by her shirt. She had avoided further humiliation by shifting her chair backwards barely half a foot.

Tears were in the mother's eyes, and he, now standing to his full height, had rediscovered the gallant gentleman in himself – the one he had only recently mislaid. He grabbed his wife in a restraining embrace which was not devoid of genuine affection. "She is our guest, as you have rightly pointed out. We must always maintain our civilised standards. We must never be dragged down to the level of those who unfortunately cannot share them."

His magnanimous speech was only partially successful in abating his wife's fury, although it did deflect whatever part of her criticism had been directed at him.

"She was attacking you, Dick," she said querulously. "She despises everything we stand for – the way we live and the way we think. She's perfectly entitled to her opinions, but would I go to her mother's house and say such things?"

Now he was enjoying his role of bounteous arbitrator. "Miss Kristina is our guest," he repeated, "and we must not only allow her to speak, but also listen and try to understand her point of view, however intolerant she is of us. Children, please take note – this will be an important lesson for you. We are a liberal nation, and if that means we're occasionally put upon, then so be it. It's a price worth paying."

"Enough," she said, having finally suppressed the agitation caused by the mother's failed attack. "Maybe I was too personal about you and your children, and I apologise for that, but your husband infuriated me with his insinuations."

"Mum, what's wrong with being a planet?" asked the eldest girl, and a titter communicated itself around the table, leaving a smile and alert eyes with each child. The adults, however, had broken through too many of their taboos to reconcile themselves because of childish ingenuousness. There was a long silence interrupted only by the occasional suppressed but expectant giggle.

She was the one who eventually broke it. Never given to talking down to children, she was utterly rational in her explanation: "It's a matter of relativity. Planets are huge, but relative to the sun they are small and dependent. That is why your mother took offence. And she was right to do so. I apologised."

There were half-smiles and exchanges of glances, as the children assessed the peculiar situation they found themselves in. They sensed the tension, but equally felt that this was a much more interesting lunch than usual. It was then that she realised that she may very well have missed out on something in her small family: not the father but the siblings. She may have missed the complicity and rivalry of childhood – the sheer emotive nonsensicality of growing up with dissimilar creatures sharing an identity and a roof. Parents would be like gods who intervene randomly and arbitrarily in the lives of children, distant figures who must be placated, humoured and very occasionally remonstrated with. So different from the very close and intense but also coldly rational relationship she had had and indeed continued to have with her mother.

Her mother was her friend and they shared everything, including their most intimate thoughts. When she was very small, things had been difficult financially, and her mother could not afford to return to Sweden. Her mother was determined not to work full-time, but they managed. Once she went to school, her mother returned to her career as a research chemist and was thereafter committed to staying on in southern England. Interesting people started to visit their small flat: artists, writers, actors, musicians, free spirits, incomprehensible drunks and the occasional academic. Her mother was involved in none of these activities, but acted as a conduit between them, always smiling, always open to new ideas, always wanting to help these people make their careers. And she was at the centre of it all, because everyone sensed the mother's priorities: no one was more important than the daughter, not even those of them who became her mother's lovers. They, in particular, understood that the daughter tacitly exercised some kind of veto. She grew, therefore, in the midst of ideas and love, both genuine and interested. What more could a child want? Whatever she lost was more than compensated for. And yet she noted his children's camaraderie and it pleased her.

"Do you often get into trouble?" the same girl said. Clearly she provided the entertainment.

"All the time," she laughed, "it's my profession. You can get all kind of jobs these days."

"Shut up, Pandora," said the mother, angered by her daughter's fraternising, "I'll speak to you later."

He, who could have made a career on stage, had adopted the posture of an imperial leader negotiating with quarrelsome natives. "Kristina, I invited you here because I was thinking about funding your play. A few niggles needed to be discussed in an open and friendly fashion. Particularly your characterisation of the single mother – of course, I didn't know when we started our conversation that you are in fact the product of that kind of 'family', as they like to define it now. So anything I said at the beginning was quite innocent and there was no intention to offend – in any way whatsoever. I hope you understand. Unfortunately, you have hurt my wife with your incautious talk and ill-considered ideas, and have created a scene that can only have been damaging to my children. It will, of course, be difficult for you to understand this, but I am the kind of father who is deeply attached to his family. I'm afraid, Kristina, that I will have to ask you to leave."

"I very much doubt you ever intended to fund the play. I believe you invited me here to show off your wealth and archetypal bourgeois family, and to give me a lecture. Well, you got more than you bargained for." With that she turned and walked to the door, and no one said a word. Both sides were now beyond words.

And so Kristina closed the door behind her and felt not anger but relief, and a sense of being a fortunate young woman who had a life she was free to do a great deal with. She felt the smoothness of the breeze, which contrasted with the stuffiness of that great house. She breathed it too and sensed her oneness with a world she felt no need to dominate, as obviously he did. Or was he dominated by that need? Did he live, or did life's leaden desires lead him?

Living with
the Polish Count

The author of this account, Abram Davidovich Geller, fought until the end of the Civil War and did not fulfil his wish to find his White bullet until 1922, when he was fighting in the Siberian region of Priamurye. In all probability it was not a White but a foreign bullet that killed him, as Japan was withdrawing the last of its soldiers after its failed and costly attempt to secure a White puppet enclave in Eastern Russia. Dimitry Gregorevich flourished after the Civil War, and became the Professor of Russian Literature at the University of Murmansk. He disappeared during the purges of 1938 and unusually we can find no further record of him. Boris Fyodorovich Bogdanov received the Order of Lenin in 1934. The citation vaguely refers to long service to the USSR and military missions abroad, mainly in China, and also states that he was going into early retirement, which suggests possible medical problems or political disaffections. Victor Lvovich Kibalchich, survivor of French and Soviet prisons, amongst others, became a prolific writer, although some of his manuscripts were destroyed (or lie undiscovered in a Soviet archive). In 1947, he died while taking a taxi ride in Mexico City. Though isolated and purposefully discredited in left-wing circles by Soviet agents, he continued to write and participate in the muddied politics of the time. His son, the artist Vlady Kibalchich Russakov, was born in June 1920, the year after the events Geller describes, and in the forties settled with his father in Mexico, where his murals in part celebrate communist struggles around the world, but particularly those in Russia and Mexico. He died in 2005.

For most of the year our immoderate sun of the north is

parsimonious with both its light and heat, and then for a short while it blazes. During the long periods, wood in the stove is as essential as the air we breathe. Our coats are never off, and our malnourished bodies rarely washed. And yet we move and struggle and talk incessantly, unsmilingly perhaps but not without humour. "We will survive and we will rebuild," said Nadezhda Alexeyevna. Yes, we will survive, but what will we build? She was almost sure of our success; I wished that I could be.

She looked like a peasant in her soldier's uniform. This would have surprised many who had seen her presented at her first Saint Petersburg ball at the age of sixteen, four years earlier. But in effect she could have been a peasant girl. Why not? Her hands were not manly, but nor were they bony, pasty-white fingers fit only for holding the finest porcelain and pointing an accusatory finger at the timorous servitude of others. Her hands were at home holding a rifle and darkened by long exposure to the wind and sun. She was short, even stocky, but she moved with a grace that excited men. Some of her comrades-in-arms, who really did come from peasant families, had been recruited under the tsar and had stayed with their units when the army turned on him. They were not alone in being unsure as to why so much had changed and unclear about what they were fighting for. She differed from them in one other respect: their eyes were tired and seemed to be focused on a landscape far from Petrograd where family and routine, however harsh, had been left behind.

Not Nadezhda's eyes: they burnt with excitement but not fanaticism, which she disdained. There's enough of it on all sides. It was not the certainty of revolution that attracted her, but its opportunities, the most important of which was a negative one: not having to play out the pantomime of being chosen for marriage by some narcissistic prince or count whose passions went no further than hunting and getting drunk at the officers' mess. It's her tragedy I want to speak of – not her death, mind you. She was resigned to that, just as I am now to my own. I want it. To live when hope is dead would be to fall short of her great values; that's the lesson of her death, that's what makes it tragic.

I often used to ask myself whether I would survive this era of war and terror. Would I complete the full semicircle of human experience we call a generation? I doubted it, but part of me wanted to see how all this will turn out. The White bullets are many and the Whites have all the latest equipment. In my line of work, a Red bullet can be as dangerous. Of course, I scribble too much and my syntax is subversive to them all. Who knows if these words will survive in some court archive? – for bureaucrats rarely throw anything away. They delight in recording the history they think they control.

This interesting talk about the colour of bullets reminds me of our conversation some months before her death. I was explaining the problems of our revolution in a disorderly, backward and individualistic country like Russia. As usual, she found my views outrageous and fascinating at the same time. She always enjoyed our little talks.

"The problem," I said, "is that we're governed by Nature, and Nature, like the powerful, thinks in big numbers while every one of these Ivans, Matveis and Timochkas thinks like an individual."

"Does Lenin think like Nature?" Nadezhda asked.

"Of course."

Her eyes narrowed slightly, but she gave nothing more away.

"That's what they always do," I continued, sensing I had gone too far. "Even if at first they don't like to, they soon pick up the habit. They do things that would have outraged them when they were opponents of the regime. Necessity, like Nature, has stronger arms than Morality."

"Dearest Abram," she smiled, "you say interesting things, but this is not the time to say them."

"It's never the time, but someone has to act the gadfly. Gadflies serve their purpose. There's never too many of them, and they can't swat them all."

"I wouldn't count on it."

"I don't. Neither of us is going to see the end of this war. You – with all your running around and crazy heroics – will catch a

White bullet sooner or later. And I – with my big mouth and crazy ideas – will catch a Red one. Probably in a yard not far from here after a beating routinely dispensed by my neighbour's boys. But that doesn't make me any less of a communist than you are, Nadya. I was in a Tsarist prison when you were going to society balls."

"I know, I know," she replies, free from any bitterness at my reference to her aristocratic past. Middle-class communists are more easily offended by such things. "Who do you think will win, Abram?"

"The Reds, of course. But in a way, the Whites too."

"More of your riddles, Abram. Are you going to explain?"

"Our armies will defeat theirs, but their officers and officials will become our officers and officials."

"How come?"

"Simple: power and the acquisition of power comes from individual psychology. A certain kind of person will always rise to the top. And another kind of person is always going to question everything."

This time she wasn't laughing. "So it's all a waste of time, according to you. You're a cynic, Abram Davidovich, and you could destroy our morale."

"Well, I hope they put you in charge of the firing squad."

"Don't be silly, Abram. But this is not a time for doubts."

"Nadya, there were never so many doubts as we have now. Look at our soldiers: one day they're defecting from the Reds to the Whites, and the next day they're coming back again. Why do they do that if they're not uncertain? But in the end they'll stick with us, because our arrogance is not as bad as White arrogance. They're stupid, these Whites. They don't have to say now that they'll take back the land, punish the peasants and work them like dogs. They don't have to say that they'll restore the Tsar. They don't have to flog their soldiers for every little misdemeanour. The Whites will lose because they're incapable of making the slightest compromise with modernity. It is the backwardness of Russia that's driving it forward."

ALLAN CAMERON

"Oh Abram, how can a clever man like you be such a fool? You think it's a game, but it's not."

"I don't think it's a game, my girl," I cried sharply, wounded and resorting to condescension. "In a time of doubts and chaos such as this, every word is deadly serious, even when we joke – especially when we joke."

"So it's all for nothing?"

"Not at all. Perhaps if all these foreign powers had not invaded, and Russia, poor Russia, had been left alone to develop the social-ist experiment with its limited resources, it would have built some-thing more enlightened and free, but History doesn't allow such luxuries. It insists on progress and then makes it so difficult."

"It too thinks in big numbers," her eyes brightened and her mouth implied a smile.

"Exactly," I confirmed, "the insensitivity of the abstract."

"So where's the abstract going to take us?"

"Towards a communist society of course. A better society even-tually. Our sacrifices will be worthwhile, but we do need to soften the blows our leaders inflict on the people; we must tell them how the people suffer."

"But what if our leaders turn on each other as they did in the French Revolution? What if rivalries between those who lead us destroy this successful revolution of ours? Can progress be assured?"

"Nadya, the French Revolution came out of nowhere and it made its leaders after it had started. Our leaders have been work-ing and suffering together for decades. They have been moulded into one by years of humiliations. They could never turn on one another."

"Abram Davidovich, even as a cynic, you're a failure. How can you be so sure?"

"And you, Nadya, are such a good pupil; I'm no longer so sure about the colour of the bullet that'll kill you."

"Don't you worry: it'll be White. Unlike you, I know what I'm doing. I'm a soldier and avoid thinking too much about the abstract or even where we're going. I'm an avenger and the vengeance I'll

48

inflict will be against my class and myself. I leave the job of making the Revolution work to the leaders. If they fail, then the fault will be theirs and their years in a Tsarist prison a wasted effort."

Hold on, I'm telling you all about Nadezhda, and she's the one this story's about. But you need to know where I fit in and who the Polish count is. You also have to know about Alexei and a little about the Frenchman and a few others. So I must get that stuff out of the way, but Nadezhda's the one who has forced me to sit down and write it all out. She's the one who has broken my heart and made me see everything so differently.

I am Abram Davidovich Geller, and I was born in the country-side fifty miles north of Odessa. I am a political commissar in the Red Army, and I have been seconded to the Comintern to assist one of their officials, Victor Lvovich Kibalchich, whom I call the Frenchman. He is an agreeable superior, although demanding and absolutely straight. He rarely acts in a dictatorial fashion, in spite of the war, and he consults me on everything. It's true that he once looked at me a little fiercely and said, "Could you stop this business of always referring to me as the Frenchman? If I'm not a Russian, then I'm a Belgian."

"I know, but I like getting some things wrong," I replied. "I think of you as a Frenchman, so that's what I'll call you."

"Abram Davidovich, I never know when you're joking."

"I'm not joking. And I'm paying you a compliment. France is where this all started. Revolution and turning the world upside down."

He laughed when he heard me say this: "Then you're an unintentional joker. France has little left of its revolution, and it also has some of the worst prisons. I know; I spent many years in one for publishing an anarchist journal. I know why you call me the Frenchman – it's because you want to underscore my foreignness. These things don't concern me. I'm an internationalist."

"Yes, of course, Victor Lvovich and so am I," I grinned, "but I'm also a Russian and Russia is a big country. As a Russian I have to find all foreigners exotic and slightly ridiculous. My intellect tells me you're an eminent internationalist revolutionary, but my rural Russian heart tells me you're a Frenchman with puzzling Parisian ways."

"Abram Davidovich," he continued to laugh, "whoever made you a political commissar must have been off his head."

"No he wasn't," I smiled again. "But he did have a sense of humour."

We both have rooms in the same building as the Polish count, an altogether more sinister fellow. Of course we respect him, because he has suffered much for the cause. The Tsarist prison guards beat him so regularly that his jaw and mouth are permanently disfigured. He wears a moustache and a goatee, dresses well for these times, and often hides his severity and merciless intellect behind an air of jocularity. This unhappy man works incessantly and is called Felix Edmundovich Dzerzhinsky. God knows what the world will think of him in twenty years time or fifty. One day a companion of his accused him of moralism, and he briskly replied as though all truth were contained in these few words, "This is not moralism; this is history playing itself out and we are its pawns." Perhaps he defends the Revolution; perhaps he undermines it. Such are the times. His contribution to this story is primarily atmospheric. He is one of the gods – all-seeing, all-knowing and all-consuming. And he consorts with the Fates.

We rarely see him, but his presence fills the building and hangs in the air like a threat. On one occasion, Victor Lvovich and I met him on the stairs and very formally Victor asked, "How are you, Felix Edmundovich?"

He stopped but didn't look at us. He seemed to be considering a very difficult intellectual puzzle, but perhaps he was struggling to retain fading ruminations. After perhaps a full half minute he turned to Victor and his face expressed mild irritation at the banal interruption to his daily routine. "Well," he said in the clipped tone of someone whose thoughts are still racing on some other subject, "as well as can be expected." After another pause, brief but long enough for his face to brighten, he added, "But busy, busy, busy. We must get together, Victor Lvovich, and have a little chat some time. We have much in common, you and I. Foreigners both, but only foreigners like us can get a grip on this crazy revolution. What is required is zeal for thoroughness. Without it there can be no progress – no revolution. The dialectic produces one paradox after another: history has called on Russians, a people most lacking in such zeal, to carry out its greatest task." He chortled with only a hint of tiredness, as though he had said something funny – or even profound.

So much had sprung from Victor's tiny courtesy, and I doubt that Victor felt any great affinity with Felix Edmundovich. War kills not only people, but also the values that motivate them. In war, the single goal of victory overrides all other things, and most especially our understanding of what is acceptable. We all change but some more than others, and Dzerzhinsky was one of those who had changed a great deal. Certainly, that invitation was not genuine; it was a pre-war reflex still active in his febrile, war-wearied mind. Somewhere there was a memory of good manners and the realisation that his behaviour was now manic and compulsive. I doubt Victor ever dropped in on the Director of Cheka for tea and a few words about the dialectic and its paradoxes. That was something I would do – something required by the events I wish to recount.

After yet another pregnant silence, Dzerzhinsky said with a thin smile, "Good day to you, Victor Lvovich," and, recognising my presence for the first time, added, "and to you, Abram Davidovich."

That encounter showed me that Felix was in all probability being consumed and destroyed by his work. The three years since he investigated and "severely reprimanded" one of his officers for hitting a detainee must now seem to him like a century of invasions rebuffed by the faltering energies of a powerful dream. Did he look in the mirror and see the face of one of his former persecutors? Was he a good man forced to do evil for a greater good, or a bad man freed to enact his vengeful dreams? A mix of both?

Perhaps human acts are never pure, and always the product of varied and sometimes contradictory impulses. A kindness could theoretically be a pure desire to be kind or alternatively a pure desire to appear to be kind, but surely it must nearly always be a mixture of the two. The balance between them may shift, of course, and who would dare to judge the balance between good and bad in Dzerzhinsky. And to judge is to be both arrogant and vain, because we cannot know.

To speak of Dzerzhinsky is inevitably to speak of ends and means. The events of recent days have confirmed my hunch that the former can never entirely justify the latter, but those who make decisions must indulge in such calculations. They have soldiers and civilians to protect. They are responsible; they have taken on God-like duties. They're supposed to know – to see all – but they can't. They're human. They have forgotten and possibly have been forced to forget that, although we can never achieve purity as we struggle through life, we should at least seek after it, and this is our principal task.

Alexei Konstantinovich Kozlov was Nadezhda's lover. And I was her ex-lover. We had become close when we were fighting down in the Ukraine, but our love affair never had the passion of theirs. I don't know how much Alexei knew, probably everything. Relations between lover and ex-lover were cool, but never too cool, because neither of us wanted to compromise our relationship with Nadezhda, and we both knew that she could be unforgiving of "old-fashioned ways". She, we felt, really belonged to the future, while we were struggling to keep up. Alexei was a good-looking young man, I have to admit that, but I was the smarter. She always chided me for my lack of seriousness, but I could never tell her that Alexei's lack of seriousness was much more serious than mine. His derived from an almost complete lack of conviction in anything but his own pleasure. He was not made for our times. I'm not saying that he didn't run risks; we all have to. But he avoided them where he could, and he had an acquisitiveness that displayed itself in his surprisingly smart boots, and shirts we could only dream of – except we didn't. Who would care about shirts, when he doesn't know whether he'll live to the end of the week? Only a man like Alexei.

Don't get me wrong! I wasn't behaving like the jilted lover, but I knew that Alexei was taking a different kind of risk – not the kind we take with the Whites – but the silly unnecessary kind which could put her in danger too. I liked him – you may not believe me – but I liked his difference from me: his handsome face always with a ready smile for everyone, even for the Whites. I saw him give a cigarette to a White soldier we'd taken prisoner – just a boy whose unsteady hands couldn't light it. Alexei lit it himself and then stuffed it between the youngster's trembling lips. "You'll be okay," he smiled at the lad, "you're recruited to the other side. We'll see you through." I think the boy no longer cared about life and death, or smiles and cigarettes; the shock of war had broken him and he would be of little use to either Reds or Whites. Of course, Alexei would have heard all about me and my foibles from Nadya, but there were some things she could only talk to me about. Like the time she came across the White officer in no-man's-land, which is now just a few kilometres from the city boundaries. This is more or less how she described it to me. Perhaps I infer too much.

She went out into the night to position herself for sniping at the enemy once the sun came up, but as soon as she got there, she acted with her usual foolhardiness, made herself a bed of straw and lay down to sleep.

"Quite a little filly," she heard someone say as she struggled for consciousness. The first thing she saw was the muzzle of an officer's pistol pointed at her head. Her hand went up towards it but his foot came down on her neck. He continued to apply enough pressure to half choke her. "You're not going anywhere, my dear, until I've had a little fun with you, and then you're going to hell where all you Red bastards belong." He threw his pistol onto the straw some six or seven metres away, and started to undo his belt.

"Nikolai, don't you know me," she rasped. "I'm Nadezhda Alexeyevna Trubetskoy."

He stopped and looked at her face carefully, until an expression of recognition gradually passed over his own. He removed his foot and looked a little ashamed. "Nadya, what are you doing with the Reds?"

"I was trying to cross over but got lost and took refuge in this barn. I'm just a girl, Nikolai, and my upbringing was very sheltered, as you know. I was caught by a band of Reds and they raped me and forced me to enlist."

"The animals! This is the filth we have to fight against? The world has indeed gone mad. We must restore order; we must punish these people, by God! We'll inflict such terror that it'll take them generations just to straighten their backs."

"You're right, Kolya. You were always so wise. Get me some water from the stream."

Dutifully, like the polite young aristocrat he was, he made for the door, his heart contested by two conflicting emotions: the first was anguish that order in this world had been so fractured that the dregs of society could commit such unthinkable acts and go unpunished; the second elation that he, Nikolai Sergeyevich Obolensky, would be the one to free this delightful young woman from the hideous barbarity into which she had fallen through no fault of her own. He was already composing a letter to his friend, Nadezhda's first cousin, in which he would explain the circumstances of this encounter – well, most of them. Of course, he had always adored her – hadn't they all? Everyone thought Pavel Mikhailevich Stroganov would be the one to take the prize, but now fate had dealt him this great opportunity. No one was to know of what had happened to her. Such things damage a young woman's reputation, but he would let her father know very discreetly, to demonstrate how his love was in no way diminished by what she had suffered. How could her father fail to be moved by such magnanimity? Once the war was over and normality restored, they would marry in style. No, on second thoughts, he couldn't wait for this hellfire to finish. Who would have thought that that shabby, ill-disciplined army of thugs would put up so much resistance? They know they have done wrong and are fearful of the consequences – the inescapable consequences.

As he moved across the barn through a mist of pleasant, restorative dreams in which his ideals – so different from hers – became concrete in a narrative of hope, she carefully compared his increasing distance from his pistol with the fixed one that divided her from her rifle. Then she moved. The rustling hay did not matter. Her calculation was infallible. In the event, he started to turn only very slowly, detaching himself unwillingly from the sluggish viscosity of his fantasy, while still the request for water remained lodged in his mind as the purpose of his movement. In a sense, he was no longer in an abandoned and war-damaged barn in no-man's-land, but back home on the family estate, where courtesy and comfort were taken for granted. He turned not out of fear, but curiosity to see what the lovely girl was up to now.

The barrel was pointed at his thigh, and the rifle's report and the stabbing pain occupied the same instant. He fell like every soldier falls – no longer the brutal slayer of his recalcitrant countrymen, but a victim of war. His smart uniform manufactured in England was now soiled with mud on the barn floor, and his blood was darkening the blue of his trouser leg. Unlike her, he had only done what was expected of him. He had not thought about society; he had just accepted society as it was, as any sensible man should. His was the innocence of the blind. Could he be held responsible for what he could not see?

She lay on the ground where she'd thrown herself, and watched him writhing on the floor, not with relish but neither with compassion. She stood up slowly and never took her eyes off him, as a hunter might treat a fierce but wounded animal. The wound gave her superiority, but he could not be dealt with carelessly.

"Nadya, why did you do that?" he asked pathetically, more troubled by his incomprehension than by the excruciating pain in his leg.

"Quite the lad," she grinned and placed her boot on his neck, applying just the right pressure as he had taught her to do. "You're not going anywhere until I've had a little fun with you, and then you're going to the hell reserved for White guards. I imagine it as an endless waste of snow; whiteness in every direction. Very appropriate, don't you think? Not just the colour of your politics, of course – the right place for those who believe so steadfastly in their own purity and see nothing, for those who are alone in the insubstantiality of their very material existences."

What she said was so incomprehensible that he now knew she was mad, and this only increased his compassion for her. "Nadezhda, my darling, what they did to you was hideous; you have, I think, lost your mind – but not forever, Nadezhda. I understand you, Nadezhda Alexeyevna, and I'll help you. We must stand together. I love you. Always have."

For Nadya, this was an unpleasant and unexpected turn of events, which she reacted to by increasing the pressure on his neck and saying, "Who did what to me? What are you raving about?"

"The Reds – they raped you."

"I was lying, you idiot."

"Why would you lie about a thing like that? They're quite capable of it, you know."

"That's your opinion, but I seem to remember you were the one undoing your belt."

"But that was before I knew who you were," he pleaded.

Exasperated by the perfidiousness of her class, she pressed her foot down hard. "I told you a lie, because I couldn't tell you that I joined up right at the beginning of the Civil War when your backers, Lloyd George and Clemenceau, decided to invade. I had already joined the party in August 1917. I am now a child of the Revolution – not a Trubetskoy at all."

He stared at her in disbelief. "But you were such a placid girl, so well-mannered and kind. An example – I might say – to other girls who lacked your maturity and self-discipline."

"You thought you knew me," she sneered, still keeping her foot on his neck and the rifle pointed at his heart. "You clearly understand nothing, Nikolai. You feel that someone has stolen your life and that you can fight to win it back. I tell you this, Nikolai," she spat, "whoever wins this war, things will never go back to what they were before. Russia has changed, and either it will build socialism or there will be something infinitely worse than what we had before."

"Socialism, what's that?" It was his turn to sneer. "Castles in the sky! Meanwhile clerks and metalworkers wander around as though they own the world. Nadya, for Christ's sake, you come from one of Russia's oldest families. How can you disown that? You think you can run a country by waving flags and marching the streets? Your Lenin is a disturbed fanatic."

"Socialism? You want to know what it means? Then I'll tell you: education for our children, hospitals, a living wage for our working people, the right of women to do all the things men do, and without hindrance. Socialism means common ownership of everything. Socialism means changing the world, and giving everyone a chance."

"Russia may never go back to what it was," now Nikolai was angry, "but the fires of hell will dim before Russia ever resembles that utopia. The *muzhiks* will never emerge from their grime and ignorance. You fool, Nadya, you've thrown away your birthright, your people. Worse, you've betrayed your country."

"Our country? How can you say that? You who fight with the Estonians and drive those six tanks General Yudenich had as a gift from the British. You're in the foreigner's pocket, and if you win, Russia will never be more than a satrapy."

She admitted it was a stupid argument, but one she wanted to pursue. They shared a past, but their dreams could never be reconciled. He was losing blood and becoming weaker. She didn't know what to do. She was not a pitiless woman, but she was a soldier and this was war. Every minute she persisted with that pointless discussion increased the chances of her death and his rescue. In the end he cursed her. She told me it was a good old-fashioned Russian curse, as fierce as the *zamet*, the wind that stirs the winter snows of the steppes. It resolved her and she shot him through the heart.

She closed the barn door, and took out a match. And the barn stood tall in the dark, its heavy timbers must once have been some peasant's proud possession. Only close to the former capital do you find barns as formidable as these. Many men would have laboured for weeks on end to build it, and it could still serve our future state. Yet she was prepared to burn it down for no apparent reason. The matchbox was slightly damp, so she heaped straw against the wall. The first match that lit would have to do its job. Was she ashamed of what she had done? In a way, she was. She could never see anyone from her past again. Unsurprisingly, she would never be able to look Nikolai's father in the face. He was a kindly man of liberal views – very different from his son, and yet clearly of the same slightly feeble-minded mould. She hadn't known the old man well, but every time they met, his face would light up in friendly, almost loving, recognition. What shocked her more was her realisation that she would never speak to her own brother again. He was a White officer. This she had heard from a source she could no longer remember. She hadn't wanted to believe, but of course it was true. Her brother had never questioned anything, and despised their father's domestic servants, let alone the anonymous masses whose labours dressed him in the finest clothes and fed him with the best food. The rift was now utterly complete.

In spite of the damp, the first of her last four matches caught. The flames quickly climbed the wall and an explosion of light flooded into the night, whose darkness she immediately sought at a brisk trot. She moved her now heavy body with a soldier's gait, her rifle in her hand and her greatcoat flapping as a light but bitterly cold wind entered her bones and tugged at her bewildered soul. He was not a bad man, she thought. Perhaps I should have shot him through the head at the start and that would have been that. All that talk, what good could it do – especially if you're talking to a dead man? Why did I want to speak to him? Because he was from my past? Was I wanting to remonstrate with my father's people? She slackened her pace, and guilt descended on her. Then she remembered that he had wanted to rape her when he thought her to be a peasant girl. She turned and spat towards the burning wreck of the barn. "You got what you deserved, *mudak*." She ran on, determined to forget that spectre from her past.

She didn't see Alexei until the following evening, and he immediately sensed that something was wrong: "Anything happen last night, Nadya?"

"Nothing much. I shot dead a White officer."

"Not to be sneezed at," he replied. "Things could have gone worse for you, if he'd caught you."

They certainly could, she thought, but she couldn't tell him what had really happened, as it would have emphasised her previous life, which she wanted to forget. She just smiled enigmatically. He was curious, but too tired to pursue the matter.

And so she still came to me either to confess or to argue. Not an hour after she told me of that incident, I too came across an apparition from my past – my distant past. I suppose these wars are shuffling Russians as though we were a pack of cards, and you never know where you'll end up or who you'll meet. She spoke to me just before sunrise as we came to the end of our guard duty. Afterwards I walked back into the city, and, on approaching the first houses, came across a party of conscripted, middle-class men digging trenches – relaxed and seemingly still bemused that they were required to carry out such tasks. On the whole, their manner was good-natured and relations with the two militiamen in command appeared to be good. Perhaps they were confident that in the next few days the Whites would break through and restore them to their former wealth and position. More likely they knew that the Whites would bring no respite, but had decided to look on their current trials philosophically and adopt an outlook of benign and slightly superior neutrality. Not "seize the day" but "accept the day and whatever horrors it might bring". Then I stopped, incredulous to see that my brother Lev was one of the party. We greeted each other more warmly than we'd done in years. We embraced and smiled at each other like ghosts meeting up in another world. So much had happened, and each would have assumed the other to be either dead or abroad. I would have expected him to have appeared more crestfallen, and he probably expected me to appear more triumphant, standing there in my uniform of the Red Army – his superior at last, and capable of commanding the militiamen who commanded him. And there was so much between us.

A quarter of a century ago we argued and swore never to speak to each other again. But we did – after a fashion. The last time we met was by chance in a Petrograd restaurant in the first year of the war. He laughed about the miseries the conflict was inflicting on the peasantry, and was unconcerned that his country was losing ground to the Central Powers. His engineering works were doing great business and in the end the royal families of Europe would sort things out. Nothing would change. And here he was, six years later, dressed as a worker and digging for an army he must despise. Still with our arms about each other but our heads held back to focus better, we searched each other's face for clues about who our brother was or had become. I suspect that he discovered as little as I did.

We released each other from our embrace – a mix of ancient familial warmth and residual cool distrust. I was the first to speak, partly to overcome the embarrassment I felt about Lev's hard times. "I thought you'd have left the country with the others."

"What others?" he laughed. "I'm not an aristocrat who'll always find a comfortable bed, however many times he goes into exile. What could war-torn Europe do with yet another destitute Russian? Force me into the ranks of an exhausted army reduced to aimless savagery, no doubt. When peace came to Europe, there was little work and no money. I stayed here and held on at the works until the workers took it over. A year later, the lathes fell idle."

"I'm sorry to hear that," I said rather oddly. I have requisitioned more than a few factories in the last couple of years.

"Why? Once the worst has happened, it's amazing how quickly we learn to live with our new reality. My wife fled taking all the liquid assets she could lay her grasping peasant hands on." The two militiamen straightened their backs disapprovingly when they heard his remark. But he had a point; Katya, his wife, did suffer from the kind of acquisitiveness only peasants display when drunk on prosperity. "If the revolution hadn't come along, our unhappy marriage would have continued into the years of our dotage. This has given me another life – not one I would have ever wanted, but then we never know what we want or should I say what would be best for us. I do not refer, in time-worn way, to our supposed intellectual ineptitude, the folly of our greed or the tyranny of our desires, because how can we possibly know what kind of society given changes will bring? We cannot be blamed for not knowing, when we have no evidence to go by. That was always my argument against people like you: how could you know that society could be improved? There is, you'll have to grant me, a little intellectual arrogance in that certainty of yours."

"And how can you be so blind, Lev? How could you be so blind to the suffering of our people?"

"And how can you be so blind to the possible suffering unleashed by sudden change – wrought, mind, by people certain of what they're doing even when they've never done it before. Would you have your barn built by someone who'd never built a barn? And come to think of it, would you knock down your old barn before you'd built the new one? That way lies starvation. I've no idea what the future brings and I've no reason to be hopeful, but I can't say that I dislike the present. I have experienced kindness in the last few months – both kindness given and kindness received. I realise now with great regret that I wasted the years in which I could have and should have shown kindness. I could have saved lives and enhanced others, and yet I did nothing. I have no right to fear the future."

"Do you need any help?" I asked and felt like a potentate. If ever I had wished for a reversal of our fortunes, I knew in that moment that it brought no pleasure; it only revealed that all power is misplaced, even the tottering power I temporarily hold and paid for in my youth with years in prison.

"I did, but I no longer do, thank you. I am getting along just fine at the moment."

"But this!" I cried, and felt quite angry about my brother's treatment now it was clear that he had lost his hubris.

"This? Oh don't worry about this. It keeps me warm in a city where everyone is freezing to death. At least I'm not at the front. On either side! My life was a nonsense; I see that now. God knows where it'll all end up. We had it coming, I'll give you that."

Suddenly I found him less convincing. It occurred to me that the entire conversation might be an act for the two militiamen. They were leaning on their rifles and staring at him with expressions that betrayed disbelief and puzzlement. I had an advantage over them; I knew that my brother had always thought it unmanly to complain and possessed an innate talent for creating a fog of misinformation. What was he cooking up?

He must have read something in my expression, because he then demonstrated an acuteness that startled me, and I, the courageous bigmouth, have become so conditioned by our current morality that his intelligence made me think him dangerous. "I know what you're thinking," he said ominously with a dramatic sweep of his arm, which showed that he also knew what the effect of his words would be, "you're thinking that I haven't changed – that I am trying to manipulate you. I can understand that. I remember very well how I behaved last time we met. I was an arrogant fool, laughing at other people's misfortunes and feeling so secure. Never before had I felt so secure and close to where power lies. That contagious self-importance that comes from mixing with millionaires and a few minor politicians. Isn't that strange? You see, we Jews yearn for security and that too is understandable. But who has it? Not the Tsar. Not the generals. No one's safe.

"We're sons of an illiterate country miller, who slaved away for a few kopecks, and what little he had, he spent on giving us a half-decent education. I could never understand why you wanted to squander that small achievement on a lost cause. All that internationalist fervour and belief in a better world – silly, that's what I thought it, just plain silly. You brought yourself misery and you upset our parents. For what? A daydream."

"Hold on," I said, slightly piqued.

"But you were right all along – that's what I was about to say – you were absolutely right, Abram. You knew what you were talking about. And even if this revolution of yours goes belly-up," he smiled at me, damn it, "you'll still have done a great thing; you'll have shown there is another way. If you fail now or you fail in seventy years, you'll have shown that there is another way, and that'll make them change their ways – not very much perhaps, but nothing will be the same, and not only here in this starving city."

And I was none the wiser. I believe in the new morality, so I had no intention of recruiting my brother. I could slip him into the party, but who knows what mischief he might get up to. I never believe in anything wholeheartedly, so I decided to break the rules a bit: I would keep an eye on him from afar, and make sure nothing bad happened to him. After all he is my brother.

I thought about what my brother had said: that we don't know what we want. And he also implied that we discover who we are not by success or by imposing our will on people or the elements. No, we discover who we are and how to enjoy life by dealing with what life throws at us. It is our passivity that is creative; our passivity that makes us human. We Russians are eastern enough to know that, and western enough to worry about whether we got it right. We have a stupid inferiority complex in relation to the West. We should shoulder this task we've been given by history and creatively let it take us wherever it's going. We should not fool ourselves into thinking we're in control of our destiny – we should merely wonder at and delight in who we have become – the explorers of a future whose culture is as foreign to us as that of any distant land. Part of ourselves is our eternal garrulousness, our endless chatter about things that matter. That really shows that we're not a Western people; they dress up nicely to talk about the weather. Talking about abstract things is for them a waste of time and, in some cases, can damage material interests. They talk to get things done and then they talk about nothing, like peacocks on display, to reassure themselves about their precious hierarchies. The first is called "business" and the second sociability, which is amusing because their main purpose is to give away as little of themselves as possible. In the old Russia, on the other hand, there were only two kinds of person: the Tsar and the non-Tsars – or everybody else. We Russians talk to reveal ourselves and our ideas. The foreigner might think it impractical, but I think it is a kind of wealth – the best kind. Besides, what do Europeans know about the weather? They should come over here and try ours. Then they'd have something to talk about.

So instead of driving off the bloody Whites, we sometimes gather with the casualness of starlings at the guardroom or in an empty building, and just natter. This happened last Friday after a lull in the fighting. The commander-in-chief had been down at the front, as had the Frenchman and his pregnant wife who slept in the back of an ambulance. The casualties on the other side were heavy, but we realised that the balance was turning in our favour. We were buoyed up, but conscious that victory was not yet ours. We went back into the city and wandered into the first empty building. A White shell had landed nearby, shattering quite a few of the windows, but it would do. We found a flat in reasonably good order and lit the stove. Some of the furniture had to be broken up to feed it, and we knew that we needed warmth if we were to maintain our exuberance. Some vodka was produced but not everyone was drinking. Alexei was, and staring absent-mindedly at his boots when he felt so inclined. He sat comfortably in this existence, thinking the best of everyone as the fool he was. A handsome fool, damn it – the most dangerous thing to be. There was Boris Fyodorovich, a true hero of our youthful republic and a little less handsome than Alexei, I think. Smart, in a solid kind of way, and orthodox, but not one of those who would shun you for a trivial remark. He knows what war is about, and war primarily leaves no room for sentimentality. No matter what the cause, war is war, and the misery it inflicts entirely random. Boris is a profoundly honest man, and when he puts his energy into something, others immediately feel the weight lift off them. He took out one of the British tanks, leading an attack in which many men died, but not as many men as would have died if the tank had remained in action. Each tank is like a battalion, and now there were none: two had been destroyed by us, three had broken down and one had fallen into a river. He's educated but not really an intellectual; when it comes to making a decision that turns on a fraction of a second, then his mind is one of the best. The powerful who dream up future history rely on people like Boris Fyodorovich to implement it for them. In spite of all that has happened since, I still think him a decent man, but one who has lost his soul for this cause. When all this is over and he sees it is not perfect, he will become either a drunk or an odious apparatchik. Sitting quietly in the corner was Dimitry Gregorevich, who in the past had been a Tolstoyan and then a Socialist-Revolutionary. He is a self-educated peasant and one of the soldiers I most respect, but he is marked down for his chequered career, which I believe to be entirely coherent. Nadya was there, but acting in a more reserved way as she distrusted Boris Fyodorovich.

Initially we gossiped a bit to remind ourselves there was life beyond politics and war, and then Dimitry said in his quiet way, "We're going to rid ourselves of the Whites, you know. Their line will break soon and we'll chase them all the way to the Estonian border. Then we'll find out what we've been fighting for: freedom or dictatorship."

"And what exactly do you mean by freedom, comrade?" said Boris in the superior way he always speaks to Dimitry. "The freedom to enslave or the freedom to cast off our chains?"

We all laughed at Boris's simplicity. "Come, come," said Alexei provocatively, "you'll have to do better than that. Dimitry Gregorevich wants to ask whether we are building a society in which there is honest and open debate in the soviets or just rubber-stamping of decisions by a new elite. It's a good question. Given that every day we risk our lives for this new society, why shouldn't we ask ourselves about what it will be like?"

Now Boris laughed and he has a brash sarcasm: "Comrade Alexei risk his life? He would have to risk his boots first."

Now we were laughing at poor Alexei, but he didn't seem perturbed. Boris, now on the attack, thought he would have a go at me. "Why don't we ask the political commissar?" he said. "Surely it's his job to know these things."

I wasn't rattled, of course, although aware that Boris would monitor my words. These things are meat and drink to me; I talk of little else. "The definition of freedom changes from one society to another, as Boris implies in his very cursory analysis, but it's not just about the constrictions imposed on us by organised societies. Freedom in capitalist society is the freedom of money to circulate primarily in its own interest, that is its value as signifier. The workers and peasants know they're not free under capitalism, because every day they experience the brutality of its limitations. The middle classes delude themselves that they are free, but they're only free to spend their mediocre wealth which never satisfies their oppressive desires and ambitions. They're no more free than a cow chewing grass in a field. The animal thinks it's free as it endlessly repeats that action of noisily tearing up a hundred blades of grass with each bite of a powerful mouth that conceals a bloated, calloused tongue. The cow doesn't know that its life is predestined. The peasant is its god who organises which meadows it must graze, where it must roam and which bull will service it. The cow has no consciousness of its lack of freedom, so it has perhaps a happy existence. That is until the peasant wields his heavy axe, the one that cuts deep into the back of the cow's neck, dispatching it almost painlessly to the dinner table."

"So the tsar is the peasants' god?" Boris asked triumphantly.

"Not at all. You've understood nothing as usual. The tsar enjoyed no more freedom than his aristocrats, his middle classes or the workers and peasants themselves. He was trapped by the trappings of power. He could not do what he wanted, because always, always he had to behave like a tsar. He couldn't control his wife, his courtiers or his mad monk. No, no, the god of us all used to be tsarist autocracy. We danced to its tune even when our legs were so tired we could hardly move them. We haven't really imprisoned the tsar; we have liberated him from the gilded prison of his office."

"I've heard that he has been executed by firing squad," said Nadya.

"Like I say, we've liberated him."

"But his family must weep," Dimitry objected.

"That goes without saying."

"I know, I know. In all the Russias, the people are bleeding and losing their loved ones daily," Dimitry smiled, anticipating the pleasure of provoking Boris and perhaps Nadya. "But as I heard you describing so lucidly and cleverly how he was not in control of his actions, like a cow grazing in the field, then I couldn't help thinking – you'll forgive me, comrade, if I'm wrong – that he couldn't then be held responsible for taking us unprepared into that crazy slaughterhouse called war."

"In a manner of speaking, you're right," I admitted after some hesitation.

"It strikes me, comrade, that freedom... I'm only saying this because you haven't yet defined freedom; you've only partially explained what freedom isn't," Dimitry continued to provoke. "It strikes me that freedom is like a cow going mad, as the peasant would see it, and attempting to go and graze a meadow other than the one the peasant chose. Or rather, if we can put the metaphor to one side for a moment, freedom is wilfully taking action not in one's own interest but in the interests of justice and human solidarity, as we understand them. And that's the problem. How can we know that we have understood them correctly?"

"People like you can come close to the truth and appear to talk sense, only to let the truth slip from your fingers at the last moment," I said, acting fully my role as political commissar mainly for Boris's benefit. "You must never qualify your thoughts with expressions like 'as we understand them'. Perhaps one day in the future we'll be able to use such debilitating expressions in our speech. They don't belong to our virile Russian workers or peasants who hold consciousness of their lack of freedom under the autocracy firmly in their heads."

"And it's only because I know it's very difficult for you to shake off your clouded, petit-bourgeois thinking, that I don't wield the heavy axe," Boris attacked Dimitry more aggressively. "But if you continue to speak like that, someone else will."

There was an uncomfortable silence until Dimitry said, "I take that as an argument in favour of dictatorship after the war."

Boris appeared to back off, and Nadya, always the conciliatory one, suggested, "It is too early to discuss exactly what freedoms should be re-established once we've driven off the invaders, but I think comrade Abram Davidovich should continue to elucidate us on the nature of freedom."

I hate it when she calls me comrade; it bureaucratises a relationship founded on real friendship. Come to think of it, I detest the term in all its uses, even though I am obliged to use it often. When I hear the word "comrade" used as a term of address, I immediately expect it to be followed by some form of mendacity – a simple lie or, worse, moral blackmail. And there was something mendacious about her behaviour, and the motivation, I believe, was her desire to protect Alexei. Whenever Nadya failed to live up to her own moral code, it was usually because of her generous nature. I felt her discomfort and decided to oblige with a little more wordiness on my part.

It was time to reassure Boris and return to the new conformity. It still feels strange to be working for the government, rather than against it. A government very different from the previous one, but a government nevertheless. Governments do governmental things, and dissidents do dissenting things. These are two very different worlds, and when a revolution comes along, you have to leap from one to the other, like leaping onto a departing vessel: you have a fraction of a second to decide whether you want to remain on the seemingly solid jetty or take a turbulent trip to an as yet unknown destination. Or perhaps it's even more dramatic and irreversible, like moving into another life and being uncertain whether you have ended up in heaven or hell. So I came out with all the truths we had accepted long before: the ever-increasing polarisation between rich and poor in capitalist society, the increasing concentrations of capital that become monopolistic, global imperialism, the perfidious foreigner who believes he has the right to decide our future. I covered a great distance in little depth, as I might do with a group of newly recruited peasants. Boris listened appreciatively as a child might listen to a well-known fairy story – not that Boris is a child or a fool; he is quick-witted and has a good practical intelligence, but he is a failed seminarist and failed poet – can you have a more dangerous combination? Dimitry Gregorevich lay back on the couch where he was sitting alone. But he could not relax and shifted his position incessantly, as though tortured by my platitudes. Nadya, on the other hand, was quite at ease and occasionally lit a cigarette. I am certain that she didn't listen to a word I said. Alexei's behaviour was not that different, but then he never listens.

"Excuse me, Abram Davidovich, if I butt in," Dimitry could take no more, "but aren't we talking about freedom? Or is our political commissar trying to bore us into going on a suicide mission against the Whites? If that's the case, I volunteer immediately."

Nadya laughed and spluttered on her cigarette smoke, and Boris said, "Take no notice of them, Abram Davidovich, they're only happy if they're ridiculing the party. You sometimes wonder whose side they're on."

Perhaps I had got carried away. I rummaged around in my brain for a suitable platitude to end my speech with something about freedom. I poured myself a small vodka and gulped it down. "Absolute freedom," I said, "can only be a state of mind and can never be granted by society, which must impose laws. By definition, all laws restrict our freedom. They may do so for very good reasons, but they are still restrictions. Our freedom is not just restricted by social coercion, but also by the failure of our own imaginations and education. Indeed the impositions and punishments inflicted by society often teach us how to be free. As someone who has spent over five years in Tsarist prisons, I can tell you that they were my finest university. You'll think I am talking about our camaraderie and reading clubs in prison, which in part I am, but I am mainly talking about the periods of solitary confinement, beatings and torture, which either break you or break you free. After that, material luxuries have no worth. Selfish desires have no worth. Fear is gone, and the heart and mind are free. We may voluntarily subject ourselves to the discipline of party or army, but we never again delegate our intellectual curiosity to others."

"Dear God," Dimitry rasped disapprovingly, "do we all have to go to prison and suffer beatings and solitary confinement to obtain freedom? Abram, that's positively medieval. We should all join a monastery. Come come, Abram, there must be some other way we can train our brains without indulging in such barbarity."

"Of course, Dimitry, you're right," I panicked and could no longer think of my feet. "Literature is one path to that kind of freedom," still very much in didactic mode, I then unwisely added, "I'm not talking, of course, of popular literature, but of high literature – our great classics."

"There are no such things as high literature and low literature," said Dimitry glumly, whilst staring at the ceiling as though he were speaking to himself or rather had no expectation of being understood.

"Oh yes there are," said Boris, brightening at the chance to say something contradictory, "low literature covers all the books I understand and high literature the ones I don't. Low literature is full of common sense and language as we speak it, while high literature tries to be fancy and uses obscure language to peddle capitalist ideology."

"If you don't understand it, how do you know which ideology it peddles?" said Dimitry, sitting up on his couch and staring at Boris fiercely.

"I understand enough of it," said Boris, and then noticing that his audience was unconvinced, he added, "and I've heard it from others – people who know about these things. That's good enough for me."

"You might as easily say," Dimitry continued, "that low literature uses a faux demotic language to manipulate the minds of working people and high literature uses elaborate language to subvert established ideas. It is much more complicated than that, of course, and European societies have learned that subversion is acceptable to the ruling class as long as it is obscure. But complex

ideas always are to some extent. That's why I reject these categories. So-called low literature is propaganda, and so-called high
literature is just literature, and the working people should not be
tricked into thinking it's not for them. Tolstoy made me a communist, not Chernyshevsky."

Everyone laughed. Alexei said, "Dear Dimitry Gregorevich,
why do you call yourself an ex-Tolstoyan?"

"Leave the man alone," I said, although I too was laughing.
"Dimitry Gregorevich is right on all counts. It's precisely because
he's right that we find him ridiculous. You see, he has thought
about it and we haven't. Besides, another thing should be made
clear: there's no need for Dimitry to renounce his Tolstoyan past;
he can be a Bolshevik and carry that past within him. Look at the
five of us, consider just how diverse our backgrounds are. The
Red Army is a motley crew, and that's our strength. This idea that
creating a new society means creating a uniform new society is our
fundamental mistake, and arises from the terrible sacrifice we're
having to make. But if we throw away our diversity of opinions,
then we throw away the new society."

"Nonsense," growled Boris, genuinely upset by my assertions.
"The common purpose that holds us together in our fight against
the Whites will be needed in fighting the economic war against
ignorance, poverty and nature itself."

"Yes and no," I said, very concerned about how far I could go,
even amongst friends. "People talk of a new soviet man or communist man, but I would prefer to say a new soviet society or a
communist society, which does not express a uniform type, but the
same diversity that must be found in any society. A society devel-
ops through the workings of its intricate variegations, which give
it robustness and flexibility. A society of uniform types will either
overreach itself or wither, or rather it will wither because it has
overreached itself and, by so doing, exposed its weaknesses. We
five are so different and yet we can make a coherent fighting force.
A common purpose does not presuppose a common essence."

"Abram Davidovich is right," said Dimitry. "And literature
teaches what he says. Literature delights in the diversity of human

types, but does not always deny equality, which is another thing. Equality does not mean all people are the same, merely that each life has the same value. The mathematical genius and the peasant stunted by lack of food and continuous beatings are equal in that they both need to eat, to be clothed and to be sheltered; each needs physical and mental exercise commensurate with their abilities; each needs love and respect. A society that can provide those things is a good society, and one worth making sacrifices for."

"Ah, the simplicity of the autodidact," cried Boris, his contemptuous smile full of confidence.

We admired Boris, but there were times when he united us against him. This was one. Dimitry is far from simplistic, and his education, which would be remarkable in a bourgeois, is quite extraordinary in a peasant. Boris, the bourgeois communist, may be willing to admit that Dimitry has done well in difficult circumstances, but he fails to see that Dimitry surpassed him long ago. Dimitry has one of the best brains in the unit, anyone who is impartial would recognise that. We sat in silence and Boris's smile died on his lips. As it did so, I realised that he was one of the most complex and inscrutable people I've known. I could not judge him because I could not understand him. I was aware that he hid within himself some unpredictable forces, which related to his competitive spirit and an overarching desire to be loved. How and why these restless spirits exist is difficult for a country boy like me to understand: I think they have what Nietzsche defined as the will to power. Such spirits only rarely achieve their narcissistic aims, but I fear that across the hundred of thousands under arms, there are quite a few of them who perceive a chance to become new Napoleons.

Boris is not the type to back off: "Are we interested in Dimitry Grigorevich's point of view, just because he's a typically vain intellectual – albeit a peasant one. You know the sort, he likes to analyse things and come up with quirky views." I started to interrupt, but Boris silenced me. "Be quiet, Abram Davidovich, you're no better. Dimitry thinks this makes an impression, but these are not times for clever talk. People suffer. Everyone suffers. And they all hold on and suffer for the different futures they dream of – not for themselves, they're too realistic for that, but for others, for society and even for generations yet to be born."

"Boris, you dislike differences of opinions," I said, "but you fabricate them where none exist. We know about suffering and we know about our times. We are the generation that has to pay the price for progress – for the future, for history, if you like. It's our best chance yet and we're so nearly there. We mustn't falter and we must continue to fight. But are our intellects so empty that we cannot ask ourselves what it is we are about to create?"

Boris took offence: "My intellect is not empty."

"Did I say it was?"

"In so many words."

Nadya stood up. "I'm off," she said, "I've things to do. Don't come to blows, comrades. Save them for the Whites." She left with her aura of tempered briskness and the others then shuffled out with a few references to our relative success on the front, our hopes, our fears, but the atmosphere was stiff. Boris can do that. We felt threatened by a friend – a suggestion of what was to come.

Two days later, Nadezhda ran to my room, which is a tiny airless space almost entirely filled by a single bed with a straw mattress. The only light comes from a small oblong window that can be opened with a rod. It must have been the bedroom of one of the more senior household servants, when the building belonged to its aristocratic owner. I was stirring after an all-night session of the international committee and no more than three hours' sleep. My first reaction was one of irritation at this interruption so early in the morning when I was just getting my thoughts together and trying to plan my day. I didn't even greet her, but nor did she.

"It's Alexei. You'll never believe what he's done now," she said without waiting to catch her breath.

I knew I would believe it, as the mention of Alexei in troubled circumstances was something I had long been dreading. My concern, of course, was more for her than for him, and on hearing his name, I changed my attitude, invited her to take the only chair and asked to explain everything from the beginning.

"So what has he done?" I asked, as I sat down on my bed and removed from the only chair in the room the report I was writing for the People's Commissariat for Political Education. As I turned to her, I gestured to the unsteady chair and gave her my full attention. It was immediately clear that she was rattled and, given her coolness in almost all circumstances, I was alarmed.

"It's so silly, I'm embarrassed to tell you, Abram Davidovich."

So embarrassed that she used my patronymic in private conversation. "Start at the beginning, but first take a seat," I said, and my tone too was rather formal.

"I'd rather not. I was looking for the wise political commissar, not for the regimental psychiatrist."

"As you wish."

"Well, it was my birthday yesterday," she said and paused, as though this was significant.

"Sorry I forgot about it," I said not without a hint of sarcasm.

She drew in her breath and, ignoring my statement, continued, "Alexei – well, you know what Alexei is like, so effusive and, well, loving, I suppose you'd have to call it that."

"Not like your previous lover – a broken old man, I seem to remember."

"Abram," she barked, not having entirely lost her aristocratic ways, "this is serious, and I'm relying on you."

"Then get to the point," my response was abrupt and betrayed my increasing impatience.

"Well, it seems he wanted to get me a birthday present. Oh Abram, I'm so embarrassed."

"Get on with it."

"He wanted to get me diamonds."

Then I understood. This was Alexei at his maddest: the world is falling apart, we're fighting a difficult war with inadequate equipment and expertise, and the stakes are very high, and what was Alexei thinking about? Buying his girlfriend diamonds, and no doubt telling himself, "What's the harm in that?" Part of me said he was not entirely wrong, and the other part said what a waste of precious time and effort, and what a foolish risk to run.

"So somehow he got hold of diamonds on the black market."

"No, he couldn't find any or, more probably, he couldn't find any he could afford."

"Thank God for that! But what was he thinking?"

"This is the really humiliating part of the story: he wanted a gift worthy of a princess. I lost my temper with him – told him that I *was* a princess and that the rest of my life will be about shaking myself free of that odious title."

"But he didn't mean 'princess' in that sense," in my relief I wanted to come to Alexei's rescue; "he meant 'my loved one', 'my treasure'."

"You never called me any of those things."

"Not my style... You have to understand that for Alexei, a working-class boy from Orenburg, the word 'princess' has no reality outside a fairy tale and fairy tales were not part of his upbringing. He would have bought you diamonds if you were a peasant's daughter, and he'd still have called you 'princess'," I laughed. "Is that all you came to tell me?"

"Of course not. He's been arrested. He may have given up on the diamonds, but he bought some silver cutlery – you know the kind, French eighteenth-century..."

"No, I don't, and I don't care."

She blushed. "It's all so stupid. I told him, 'What do I have to do with silver cutlery? Can these knives peel potatoes or cut our heavy rye bread? Won't this exquisite spoon argue with the tin bowl I use for soups? Will this delicate fork pierce the occasional cut of tough meat that happens our way? These things are not just for another time; they are for another society – one that we have overthrown and should erase from our minds.'

"And he replied, 'Why? Is it illegal to be fascinated by the intricacies of beautiful objects? I'm not asking you to eat with them; I'm asking you to put them away for better times. Why should we erase our past; it belongs to us. We may despise Tsarist society, but it's part of us and will stay with us for as long as we live. Besides, bad societies create good things as a reaction against them. We may create a fairer society, but will we be better people? Will the plenitude of our Soviet society create the 'new man', the new selfless man? More probably it will produce a race of self-confident and selfish people. We have overthrown Tsarist society. Good. But we'll always be its children, the last of its children.' What can I do with silver cutlery in the middle of a war – even if I wanted to?"

"Probably sell them on. There's a whole economy of currently worthless things circulating around the city, and mainly they are a means of storing one's wealth, when most things can't keep their worth. The more useless they are, the more useful they become for storing one's wealth in portable form, although a few silver spoons aren't going to get you across many borders."

"Exactly, so why arrest him?"

"Because it's the law."

"And shoot him?"

I jumped off the bed and stared at her, as the horror worked through my limbs and insinuated itself like a nauseous disease. I wanted to hold her, but was frozen by a state of despair that will never wholly leave me. For her to lose Alexei at the front would have been hard, but also half expected. To lose him in this way – I knew what pain that would cause her.

She started to cry, but immediately felt ashamed of her tears. "I wouldn't cry, if it weren't so silly…"

I now knew why she was here in this building: "I'll speak to Dzerzhinsky as soon as I can. Don't hope too much of that man, but I'm sure he's not a monster." I put my hand on her shoulder at last, but I knew that those words of mine were all she wanted and then for me to act on them.

I left the room without saying another word and leaving her with her tears.

Dzerzhinsky's office was not large, and two of his assistants were at work there too. He greeted me very cordially and listened to my story. "Strictly speaking," he said, "your friend has broken the law, and should be punished."

"That severely?" I protested, "after fighting bravely to defend our city?"

"Listen, Abram Davidovich, I have just recommended the death sentence for an old comrade of mine. We were picked up in Warsaw together, spent time in prison there and then a terrible period in Siberia. He fell for a woman who works for a White spy ring in this city. He was absolutely loyal, but his indiscretions have cost lives. An affair of the heart. Very sad. But the law is the law. We can't make exceptions for our friends and relations."

"Of course not, but a few knives and forks?"

"I understand your argument," he relaxed and smiled at me, "and it seems unduly harsh, but the black market is a serious problem for us. Abram Davidovich, I admire you as a loyal comrade of many years' standing; I have to listen when you speak. Indeed, you can tell ... what was the name of the lady comrade involved?"

"Nadezhda Alexeyevna Trubetskoy."

"Isn't that an aristocratic name."

"I think it may be, Felix Edmundovich," I replied without mention of his own aristocratic blood.

"No matter, you can tell her that I will sort this one out. Let's see if we can resolve it with a happy ending. So many deaths, so much misery."

Again I jumped to my feet, this time with joy, and I shook his damp hand energetically. That was one of my many errors in this whole affair. I should not have let him see my emotional attachment to those young people – or to Nadya really. Perhaps he smelt a rat. It is his job to have a suspicious mind.

Nadya was delighted and abashed – the affair had undermined her identity as a soldier in the Red Army. She had been dazed by the turn of events, but now he was safe, she found room in her heart to be furious with Alexei. "There is something profoundly petit bourgeois about Comrade Alexei," she said to me stiffly. "I can't thank you enough Abram; you've always been such a good friend ..."

In that moment it felt like we were two people who had never made love. Strangely that didn't matter to me. I felt her pain as though it were my own, and although such pain is real enough, it is accompanied by a slight exhilaration at that momentary escape from oneself. But my relief was qualified by my reliance on the Polish count. She, the dedicated communist who generally thought only of the war, was now completely consumed by her desire to be reunited with her lover – presumably to start with a vicious scolding. I felt once more that my presence was not required and left like a theatregoer numbed by a particularly effective tragedy.

The snow was thick underfoot and it slowed my pace. Then I realised that I was hurrying without any great purpose. Yes, there were things to be done at the Comintern office, but I had no desire to do them. I relaxed into the slow trudge the snow imposed on me, and made my way there primarily for the relative warmth, though we rarely remove our coats. I felt the cold in my lungs and I felt the number of my years. The exertions of army and administration on a poor diet with little sleep were ageing me. The shock of Alexei's arrest seemed to be draining my last reserves and demolishing my hopes. Those hopes had started in my youth along with my outrage against the times: I joined Emancipation of Labour in 1887, the Russian Social Democratic Labour Party in 1898 and the Bolshevik faction in 1903, shortly before I was imprisoned for treason. I was restricted to minor duties, in spite of my long service. No surprise there: I was always a faction of one, disdaining to exchange my intellectual independence for a career. The 1905 Revolution led to my being amnestied by the regime, and my arrest in 1910 on conspiracy charges was rewarded with detention in Siberia until my escape in 1913. And in all those long years, I have worked and struggled with barely a thought for myself, and always always I have been talking about a possible future that seemed as real and feasible as it often felt distant, but now we have a victory that we must defend at any cost – and that victory, more than Lenin or Trotsky, is our harsh dictator. We have to keep fighting, not so much to move forward, but to avoid falling into the abyss of the past.

Rarely do our lives enmesh with our times and the past is like a continuously changing vanishing point swallowed or reduced to nothing by the lines of perspective. Our finite and travailed stories cannot cohere with the endless unfolding of history, the god that never fails never to feel. Perhaps, I thought, the young – like Alexei and Nadya, if they survive – will live to see our economy improve and real benefits for our working people, but I will not. Perhaps the Whites will win and cobble together a dictatorial state run by one of their monstrous generals, who after victory will fight amongst themselves. Blood will flow and the *muzhik* will pay for his disobedience to established order. Suppose they forget to imprison me, will I in twenty years be trudging these same streets through the winter snow in a White capital, and muttering to myself about half-forgotten ideals no one dare mention? Passers-by will laugh and some fat bourgeois will press a few kopecks into my hand on his way to church to thank the Lord for supporting the righteous. Worse: I will accept the paltry sum, my spirit broken by hunger and want – the two devils by which the rich hold their power while telling you you're free.

The next two days passed quickly, like most others. We are accustomed to dropping one task and rushing to another. We're building a new world, but we're doing it on a shoestring. The Frenchman came in and I gave him the good news. He smiled and said, "Abram, you have a good heart."

"No more than you," I replied.

"Oh I don't know. I feel they've drawn me in too far. Things are happening that shouldn't."

"That's war – even war to free mankind."

He didn't seem very happy with my answer – or even interested in it. "Of course, we have to continue, but this war is changing us. Is it changing us forever?"

"Possibly."

"Could it be that in these wars, winners could be losers and losers winners?"

"Not exactly. But it's true that in victory the victor always has to concede something to the defeated."

"Such as?"

"Not only will we have to grant jobs and privileges to much of that great mass of Tsarist officials the Whites recruit from, we will also have to allow the peasantry to be peasants – to own their land and sell their produce, because they know how to do it and we haven't even invented the replacement system. In the meantime we have to eat."

"Never. I cannot accept either of those things."

"That's because you're an ex-anarchist, and have never understood the very practical necessity of creating another state."

"You're a bit of an apparatchik, Abram."

"Not at all, Victor Lvovich, apparatchiks repeat the current fashionable truth – not next year's and not last year's."

"I take it back, Abram Davidovich, you're an excellent political commissar. Would there were more like you. We're stifling the revolution and the war provides a good excuse."

"Wars always do. It's sad, though, to see that we act like any other state."

"Abram, I'm losing my conviction that we can ever be free. If such a revolution as ours has already ..."

"Ah freedom again," I said wearily. "We all know what it is, but no one can define it."

"This is true of most important things. Often we can only define them by what they're not."

"So I've heard, but however elusive its definition, we all feel we would recognise its physiognomy, if it appeared before us. We're probably wrong. We want a world in which things are consistent with the categories we have invented for them. For us, communism means freedom and social justice, and for the Whites, it means disorder and denial of the natural hierarchy of human society, but we have to admit that communism is not wholly freedom and social justice, just as the Whites have to admit that we're not disorder, as we're proving on the battlefield, and sadly we're not entirely devoid of hierarchy. We and the Whites are radically different forms of order, but we both contain within us a chaos of different personalities, visions, rivalries, hatreds, ambitions, opportunism, hopes, courage, generosity, inconsistency and all other human foibles. There is something heroic in our attempt to go beyond ourselves and control our fate, and there is also something vain and foolish. I would like to think that in us communists there is more of the former and less of the latter, while in the Whites there is almost only the latter. They're desperate to recreate an ideal past they can never return to, and we're desperate to create an ideal future we will perhaps never reach."

"Abram, are you a dreamer or a cynic? What you've just said is cynical in the extreme."

"Not cynical, just realistic. To desire the good of humanity is noble, but to think it easy to define that good is foolish and to consider the achievement of that good, once defined, to be something routine and painless would be almost criminally insane."

The Frenchman smiled and said, "We mustn't lose heart. There can be no progress until this damn war is over. Then things will change, you'll see."

"I hope so, Victor Lvovich."

In that moment one of the Frenchman's secretaries ran in. "Alexei Konstantinovich has been shot."

We didn't move as we struggled to understand.

"By firing squad," she clarified.

Still we didn't reply.

"But there's worse for you, Abram Davidovich. Nadezhda Alexeyevna knows and is at this very moment rushing to prison. She's not in control of herself. Only you can calm her."

"You'd better go," the Frenchman told me.

"I don't need you to tell me," I rose wearily from my chair, still vainly trying to comprehend Alexei's death – hardly an event in a world where so many die needlessly, inexplicably and unnoticed.

The Frenchman's secretary touched me on my back – a slight and timorous act of solidarity, a gesture of compassion, where compassion seems a luxury. I had lost many friends in this war, and Alexei was not a real friend; he was however something more, a member of a fragile ménage of emotions whose purity kept me sane. I stumbled into the street and had to force myself to quicken my pace towards the prison. Driven by duty, I dreaded my arrival.

On my way, I saw my brother's work party sauntering off towards their duties. I put my head down, intending to hurry by, but Lev broke out from their ranks and rushed over to me. He hugged me more forcefully than at our last meeting – with a needy intensity. I understood the difference: the other day his embrace had been one of genuine fraternal warmth on seeing a familiar face, while this was not so much an embrace as an attempt to grasp onto a means to physical safety – I was his life-belt. Why the change of mood since our last meeting, I asked myself. Most probably, Lev being Lev, he had been organising some kind of deal. Wherever he goes, he leaves a trail of financial transactions that usually leave him the richer and others he's met the poorer. This one was probably predicated on his absolute belief that before long the Whites would be in the city. "Comrade," he said, and that word made me shudder, "I was most affected by our recent conversation."

"Did we say that much?" I kept my distance.

"Oh yes, we said a lot of things and, besides, I have been thinking about them for a very long time. A man can realise that he was wrong, you know. I'm not as stubborn as you think. I have expertise – I know how the system works."

It was all a little garbled, but garbled statements often give you a very clear idea of where a conversation is going. I felt tired, overwhelmed by my own troubles, but this man's presence had just enough pull on me to keep me standing there. "So what have you decided?"

"I must join the party I should have joined decades ago. Abram, you must forgive me for all the foolish, arrogant things I've said in the past. But at least you have the pleasure of hearing me say this – your brother pleading and admitting the error of his ways."

"There's no pleasure in that," I said, "I can assure you. For a couple of decades, your 'error', as you call it, saved you from acquaintance with the inside of a stinking Tsarist prison. There's no need for you to join any party, you understand. As long as you haven't done anything illegal, you've nothing to worry about. And you haven't done anything illegal, have you?"

"No," he said, and the disappointment in his voice was like an accusation.

"Not playing the black market, for instance?"

"No, absolutely not," he said with even less conviction.

"Then you've absolutely nothing to worry about. Incidentally, if you have, joining the party would only make your position worse. You understand that, don't you?" By now, I was almost certain he was guilty of something, but I would not report him. There was still part of me that felt sorry for him, but others, in that moment, were placing greater demands on my compassion and my feelings.

"Of course," he replied curtly, already moving away to rejoin his work unit. I let him go, and we hurried in our different directions and towards different fates. I doubt we'll ever meet again. Of course, whatever he's guilty of will be a much bigger crime than trading a few pieces of antique cutlery – the misguided but ultimately harmless act of a man who could not live without his lover's smile, her subtle smile that expressed an intelligence he believed in like a religion. And I, too, had fallen in love with that smile and knew its power – all the more powerful because its wearer was never conscious it was there.

Boris Fyordorovich had commanded the firing squad, so Alexei died heroically at a hero's hand for a foolish gesture not devoid of extravagant generosity. The physicality of the lovemaking transcended the madness and cruelty of war. Change hurts and heartlessly destroys the most tender and beautiful things. And nature in such unforgiving times, always in search of balance and the indestructibility of every energy, allows us to display even greater acts of generosity and sacrifice. Pain gives rise to glory – not that of the battlefield, but of the stubborn goodness of many in the face of the terrible evil of the few. When so many drink to numb their nerves, why shouldn't he have got drunk on love, a less lonely intoxication. How many lives? How many questions? And still we'll fight, but without him. He was willing to fight our enemies and perhaps his, and offer his life, which we ended on a whim, a scruple and a fear of the insidious enemy – fear that like a mirror reflects the vicious foe.

I arrived too late. I should have hurried more or not at all – the dead are in no hurry. I was suppressing my anxieties about her – certain of her good sense, thinking of her survival against greater odds. I heard a shot when I was but five paces from the prison door. I continued in a daze. And there she lay in a pool of blood, while no one knew what to do. This was not just another corpse; something of her nobility made her dead body unapproachable. No, I'm not talking about aristocratic nobility – that's a false coin she had rejected unreservedly – I'm talking about human nobility which can be found in any class and in any people and in any part of the globe. She lay dead as she had lived, utterly coherent with her own invented values, a lesson to us all. This was not the way it was supposed to be: she was to get the White bullet and I the Red. I'll get myself transferred permanently to the front. That'll please the Polish count: I met him on the stairs shortly after Nadya's death and challenged him about it. He shrugged his shoulders and raised his forearms with hands upturned, as though to say, "What can you do, these things happen," but what he actually said was more dismissive: "I must have forgotten. We're at war, if you haven't noticed, and I've got a lot on my mind." Yes, I need to get to the front and stay there, chasing a White bullet so that we can give things their proper balance. And while I'm doing it, I'll chase those Whites as hard as I can and make the bastards pay. They're the ones who tore the heart from our revolution.

How did it happen? I spoke to everyone who witnessed her death, including the culprit, Boris Fyordorovich. The hero was defensive, clearly ashamed in my presence and perhaps a little fearful of his colleagues. No one justified what he did.

She arrived in a fury and confronted him. "Boris Fyordorovich Bogdanov, how could you kill a comrade who's fighting the Whites? Won't you need him tomorrow or the day after when we return to the front?" There was nothing of the weeping woman in the way she approached him. She had left that person behind in my room and had no intention of revealing her to Boris Fyordorovich.

"It was the decision of the court," he replied, reasonably enough.

"Indeed, but why is that silly grin of yours still on your face?" she said. Others told me that this was unfair; at that stage he was still a little defensive in her presence. She appeared to be set upon provoking him, and that's not difficult to do.

He composed himself and straightened his back even more than usual. He looked her in the eye and said with the crassness so typical of him, "He broke the law and paid the price."

"Well, that's all right, Boris, let's all go and drink a glass or two of vodka and celebrate our wonderful republic. You know I killed a man – I killed a wounded White officer."

"Well, at least you've achieved something in this war," he said, already more antagonistic.

"And that officer called our leader a disturbed fanatic and scoffed at our ideals."

"It would be surprising if he'd behaved in any other fashion. We're well rid of him."

"And are you well rid of Alexei Konstantinovich? A proletarian. A Bolshevik. A soldier who fought valiantly …"

"Valiantly, Nadya? You cannot believe …"

"Oh Boris Fyordorovich Bogdanov, you think yourself the only hero in the Red Army." Apparently he took this very badly. He was uncharacteristically lost for words, and she exploited her advantage. "The White officer said that we can't run a country by waving flags and marching the streets. I sneered at him, but when I look at you, Boris Fyordorovich, I have this horrible doubt that he could have been right."

"Nadya, does it look like we're just waving flags and marching the streets?"

"Boris Fyordorovich, yours is not a subtle mind. Where rhetoric prevails, the complexities of life are forgotten. A system that has so little flexibility that it shoots one of its own soldiers for a few knives and forks is a system that has lost its judgement."

"It's not the knives and forks," Boris said, having now regained his jocular superiority, "it's how he bought them. He must have accumulated quite a bit from his little transactions. And come to that, where did he get those boots from?"

There are many ways he might have got them, but Nadya was not interested in these legalistic arguments. She was concerned with her own concept of justice, which was as complex as it was absolute. In a time of rigid categories and simple absolutes, she held to a measured and flexible understanding of duty and personal responsibility that was a humanistic labyrinth, a culture. We loved her because she did not judge, and gave us her understanding of human weakness and generosity, but did not impose it on us.

"Boris Fyordorovich, I shot a man through the heart in cold blood – no, I did worse, I shot him while his blood was draining from his body. It seemed part of this terrible struggle for a just future. It made sense then; I don't know that it does any more. I realise now that when we kill, no matter how noble the cause, we diminish our souls ..."

"Souls? Do we still believe in such things?" Boris laughed and turned quizzically to those around him. They avoided his glance, tense and embarrassed – wishing to defuse the compelling scene that unfolded before them, and not knowing how to intervene.

"Yes, souls. We diminish our souls and can never restore what we have lost, any more than we can restore an amputated leg. But a leg is not a soul – a soul is where we store our essence, our relationship with our fellow humans. It is what makes and unmakes us. To live with an amputated limb is noble, but to drag one's body through life with a soul from which much has been severed is ignoble in the extreme."

"The ramblings, I would say, of a deranged religious fanatic," Boris smiled at each in turn, but his smile was not returned.

"Quite," she snapped, "there is a part of religion we should not have dumped so hastily; I see that now. I shot a man who writhed in pain, and now I pay the price. Revolutions must live by higher morals or die, and die they usually do. I shot a man through the heart without a sense of guilt, and now my heart longs for the Red bullet in your gun. Could you do that, Boris? – kill a woman who writhes in pain?" She pointed to her chest.

For an impulsive man like Boris Fyordorovich, who had killed many people on the battlefield and a few at firing squads like the one he had just commanded, this was an opportunity that anger and bravado would not let him pass by. Two of the five witnesses I interviewed told me that he then laughed again, while three of them had no recollection of this. In this Manichaean conflict between equality and hierarchy, it appears that we smile and laugh not for humour, joys or social niceties, but out of a dark and grieving bitterness. When we joke amicably, our expressions are often ironic deadpan.

Whether or not he laughed, he apparently said, "You mean like this?" and raised his pistol from the desk until it was level with her heart.

His hand was steady and his expression jocular. Hers was icy and unflinching. Some said that she was willing him to do it; others that she looked calm and apparently uninterested in how this encounter would end. They all agreed that fear was entirely absent. The shot I heard killed her instantly, and when I entered everyone stared as though they'd seen a crucifixion. In death she seemed more vibrant than they – like a Roman republican unwilling to live with the empire, she had fallen on her sword, and the sword she'd used was Boris Fyordorovich, a man predictable in his ambitions and reactions. A man of the future, no doubt.

I had him put in a cell for the moment – more for his own protection than anything else. Who should we blame for her death? Boris, the brutalised captain who can barely remember the ideals he first decided to give his life for? For still he risks his life, now less driven by his love of humanity than by his hatred of the many foes foreign and White, who would now restore every last indignity of the former regime and wash the country clean with the blood of those who should have never dared to speak up, let alone act. Or should we blame the gods – those eternal truths: capitalism, communism, Christianity, nation and history? These are the names we have for the winds of change that blow away the lighter, more intimate thoughts that circle in our brains. They leave us bereft of hope, even when they were the original source of it.

When on 25 October 1917 according to the old calendar we overthrew Kerensky's provisional government and sang the Internationale, we thought we had started to free the world. Now I understand that we had opened the door to a new era of struggle in which language and lies are the important weapons. This century will be fought over not only with the machinery of war – machine guns, tanks, planes, gas, wire and cheap industrial brandy – but also with lies. There were always lies, just as there were always spears, arrows and other instruments for ripping human flesh apart, but the new machinery of government will fire lies like a machine gun fires bullets. So we'll need new machinery to protect ourselves against the disseminators of lies, and that machinery will be run by people like the Polish count and Boris Fyordorovich, but eventually the disseminators and those who fight them off will become indistinguishable.

Dimitry Gregorevich was right about faux demotic language. The people are susceptible to it, recognising it as their own. But it isn't, because they have no control over it. It is a caricature of themselves, written by people who speak in a different manner, and it controls them. The Italian Fascists have led the way in this, and they will probably take power. Their usage is still crude and bombastic, but the Europeans will hone these new weapons over the coming decades. We'll always be at a disadvantage, because truth should be on our side, but this battle of sly words hurled into the wind will corrupt us.

Dimitry was a good man, if I may use such a dated and unscientific term, but his goodness was never of the emotional and impractical kind. During our retreat when General Yudenich first invaded, we were sent off on a reconnoitre to check the enemy was not trying to outflank us. We were deep in the forest and we found a soldier seated on a fallen trunk whose aged bark could no longer resist the damp and was prey to lichen and mould. He wept unceasingly. Silently and to himself. His uniform showed him to be one of ours. I was moved to help him and addressed him in a soft and, I thought, friendly voice. I shuddered at his reaction and it taught me more about the nature of war than any speech by general or politician, or any bloody encounter with the enemy in which the outcome of conflict was plainly evident to my eyes. It told me of the measureless affliction of all war, not just the deaths they count – however dizzying in their finitude – but also the chain of unnumbered consequences that ripple out across the nation and down through generations yet to come. It tells me now in the darkest moment of my life that whatever I have suffered is as nothing compared to his unknown anguish. He turned and looked at me with disdain, but his weeping became audible – horribly audible. The sound was not so much infantile as feral – a deep uncalculated protest at the calculated cruelty of our species – which outstrips the random, insensitive cruelty of nature.

I wanted to help him back to our camp, but Dimitry dissuaded me. "Be sensible," he said, "he needs food and perhaps he can survive. If we take him back, we may do him no favour. He's probably a deserter and who knows what story lies behind his presence here in the forest. He's as far away from the armies as we can get him; it's the safest place for him to be."

"Can we pass him by, like the priest and the Levite?" I objected with a frown of dismay that reflected my muddled thinking.

"You have to," he replied, "the Good Samaritan lived long before the advent of twentieth-century warfare and its excesses. But I like your source – was that for me?"

"Not at all, weren't those the stories they brought us up with, and its meaning is clear enough to me."

We gave him most of our food, and Dimitry exchanged his coat with the man. He was so stiff with cold and hunger that we had to help him remove his ragged old one and replace it with Dimitry's. Dimitry put on his, which was next to useless. Dimitry sat with him for half an hour and talked of how to live in the forest. What to eat and how to keep dry. He explained that safety could be achieved by walking towards the north in search of a remote village, and more rashly he gave him our compass. Never did the man speak, but he did occasionally nod to show that he understood.

Alexei is dead, and he was shot for his humanity. I do not speak of the grand humanity that talks of ideals and power. I speak of that quotidian humanity that delights in a good meal or a fine pair of boots. Nor do I speak of ambitious materialism, but of Alexei's innocent and entirely balanced appreciation of the materiality of life. No wonder Nadya preferred him to me and my intellectualised asceticism. I cannot conceive of a society that only thinks about material things and economic self-interest. It is a fanciful idea and would certainly be a very unhappy society, but a society that denies these for everyone and for all natures would be equally unhappy.

And Nadya is now dead. For me the Revolution died with her. For me her death and the manner of it deny the justice of our bloody cause. For me she still rises over the barricade and leads us fearlessly in a war that must go on. Whatever comes out of this will be neither fish nor fowl. At best, it will be a stepping stone to something better.

After I had informed Boris that I would have to take him down to a cell, and the room had filled with people, I had my last conversation with him: "There's a fundamental truth that you've got to learn, Boris Fyodorovich. At some stage in your life, you'll learn it – you'll be obliged to learn it. That may be in two months' time – I hope for your sake that it will – or it may be two minutes before you die at the age of eighty-three in your comfortable dacha. In that case, you'll have only two minutes to sweat the regrets of thirty thousand days – your soul will scream and your eyes will roll – and time itself will still, so that it can observe the horrible sight of a moribund struggling with the realisation that he's wasted his life."

"Really," said Boris – but this time he had difficulty in smiling the thin smile that died on his lips. "What is this profound truth you wish to reveal to me? It had better be good after such an introduction."

"Not profound, Boris Fyodorovich: this is not a debating hall. I'm not interested in sounding clever. Clever talk rarely gets close to the truth, although it does bring its own pleasures. No, not profound at all – trite, perhaps."

"Then say it. Speak as you eat, like a man who goes about his business."

"If a man has no humanity, then he is a man no more. And when he dies, he dies like a dog."

"Is that it, Abram Davidovich?" Boris laughed the most genuine laugh I ever heard resonate from his mouth. It tinkled, and I could feel it freeze the blood of everyone in that room. It spoke of our future – one I mustn't live to see. I will fight on and seek out a White bullet to pierce my broken heart.

I, the Statue

The Art of Nothingness. What can the non-statue people know of my inspiration? They are too unfeeling, too hardened in their own knowledge of life to understand the beauty of emptiness. But theirs is another kind of emptiness, now I think about it. Thinking about things is, however, something a human statue should avoid doing if at all possible. It is wasted energy. The really clever thing is to train the brain to empty itself of everything – of all the noise, anger and desire of the modern city when you're in the midst of it. Those who shout and scream their troubles to the world cannot understand the subtle sensitivity required for inanimation. The art of nothingness is the true art of being.

The equipment. Like the painter, I too have my brushes: five of them of varying sizes arrayed upon my dresser. I love these tools of my trade. They are the first things I touch when I get up in the morning. Before I shake muesli into a bowl and pour skimmed milk over it, before I put three-quarters of a teaspoon of Nescafe into a mug and switch on the kettle, and before I undress and go into the bathroom for my morning shower, I sit down in front of my dresser and count my brushes. Yes, I actually count them, as though some malign spirit, conscious of how dear they are to me, might come in the night to steal one from me out of pure, impassioned malice, which is a distillation of ambition. This is the one emotional perturbation I allow myself each day. It is like a homeopathic medicine: a tiny drop of poison that inoculates me against whatever slights the non-statue people might heap on me during my working day.

I import the makeup from Hertford University Services in

America. All those who follow my trade know of this institution, which also supplies Hollywood. Little do they know as they pass us in the street and jeer, that we're using the same products as their most favoured film stars!

But I don't apply the make-up until after breakfast. My first act in the morning is not work; it is more a prayer or homage to my metier. Once I have refreshed and restored myself with food, drink and ablutions, I return immediately to the dresser. I look into the oval mirror and study my face as though it weren't my face, but a canvas, shall we say? A canvas that has to be covered with a uniform layer of creams and powders to create a very particular visual effect. That of granite rock.

Becoming a statue. Most people think granite is grey. That is because they have never really looked at granite. They are in such a hurry to do whatever they do, that they cannot look at all the things around them. I see them every day as they rush. That is all they seem to do. Are they happy? I cannot say that they aren't, because I cannot possibly know, but if they are happy, then I am quite sure they are deluded. Yes, that is the one thought I allow to cross my brain unresisted. Even when I'm at work, I permit such things to happen, but no more than once in a shift. It's like a spark in a light bulb that immediately fuses. That thought does not clutter my brain or agitate it. No, it empties it like a vacuum. It virtually kills my brain or stuns it. My passivity requires less concentration, and my being attains a state of beautiful numbness.

Granite is not only grey; it contains bluish and greenish specks and even little cells of translucency: nascent diamonds that would have grown given more heat, more pressure and more years, but are now jostled by their greyer companions too rushed to transluce.

I didn't always do granite. There was my gold period, which I look back on as rather vulgar. We all have to develop as artists, and although I clearly have a natural talent, I had to learn the art like everyone else. Gold seemed so flamboyant and I still bore within me the last traces of the arrogant and assertive culture that hurtles round me like a vortex in which I, the epicentre, alone experience absolute tranquillity. I had not yet understood the purpose of our art, which is not a human being imitating a statue; it is a statue of a statue of a human being. It is a higher form of art than sculpture itself. Michelangelo and Rodin only studied the animate through the medium of the inanimate, but we study the inanimate through the medium of the animate and thus become inanimate. We reach a higher state of consciousness.

Gold was easy. The makeup was easy, and it only took a can of spray-paint to turn an old suit into a golden one. But gold didn't express my inner feelings very well – not the depth of my inner emptiness. When I was gold, I wasn't really a statue. I was, you might say, in a transitional state. Half-man, half-statue. Satisfactory as a direction of travel, but not for long.

One item from my gold period is still in use. It's the gold-sprayed cloth cap that serves to collect my takings. Those who appreciate my work throw coins and the occasional note into the cloth cap, and its goldness represents our terrible, oppressively inescapable necessity to get our hands on cash just to survive in this society, even if you're a statue. Of course, most of my outgoings are on the makeup imported from America, and I'm happy to suffer for my art. Those who have to paint, paint, those who have to play music, play music, and those who have to petrify themselves, petrify themselves. The artistic drive will not be denied.

So I keep my gold cap as a reminder of my journey – of how much I have achieved in a relatively short career and of how much I have sacrificed for it.

Tricks of the trade. People ask me what's the hardest thing about being a statue. Do your legs ache? What do you think about? How do you keep still? Such questions! Each one betrays their terrible ignorance. Like the tone-deaf listening to music or the inarticulate to poetry, the public stand before the human statue and think it is a game, a moment of distraction in their day. Some, the most ignorant of all, actually resent our presence on their streets. "Why don't they get a proper job?" they say. How little do they know.

Nevertheless, art is artifice, and great art makes artifice look natural and spontaneous. The first thing you must do if you want to follow this career is learn to empty your head of all thoughts. This is the hardest thing to do and requires great concentration. Not thinking is the very essence of a lump of granite, whatever its shape or likeness. Your rock-like passivity can only become credible when you have achieved a true state of emptiness. This means avoiding any stimulus that might provoke anger or strong emotions. Don't watch television and don't buy newspapers. By all means study the movements of ants in your bedsit without, of course, interfering in their behaviour. Interventionism is strictly forbidden. But don't study anything human, as it is likely to trigger animate sensations.

I live in Glasgow and work a patch in Buchanan Street. Our weather is unpredictable and one summer afternoon turned cold. As the streets emptied I resisted the desire to stop work early. My hours are fixed and usually only heavy rain will drive me from the streets. A compromise, I'll grant you, because a truly inanimate statue would disregard all the elements. As I struggled with my sense of duty, a young woman with blue hair passed by. She was short, athletic and well modelled by nature. She wore a tight T-shirt and baggy black trousers. She glided as she walked and barely noticed me. My mind filled with thoughts and sensations. My heart leapt and accompanied hers. All my senses were focused in a single direction, and my defences were down. In that second, I was hit by a moving object that brought me to my knees. A chubby girl of about eight or nine was hanging around my neck, and she was laughing with delight – the harmless delight of a child. "He's down," she shouted and others joined her laughter. Theirs was crueller. It was the laughter of adults, who are more likely to detest or at least distrust the figurative. I, the statue who had learnt perfect passivity, rebelled against it all. I jumped in the air and twisted as I did so, tossing the girl away like a stuffed toy, an object devoid of will. Even as I watched the short arc of her trajectory, I knew that I had made a terrible, inexcusable mistake. She fell badly and hurt her ankle. Her screams were unrestrained, and a second later her father's fist was in my stomach like a small rock landing on a mattress. Pain and anguish: I was a statue no longer, just a lonely, middle-aged man who had made a fool of himself. I shuffled home that evening full of thoughts, regrets, self-hate and misery. Why had I done it? Because I had broken the golden rule of statues: never feel. Or rather, never feel like a human being feels; always feel like a rock must feel, which means eschewing all human consciousness. The girl with blue hair had distracted me from my professional statueness.

That was my greatest failure, and it derived from a momentary lapse of concentration. My greatest success occurred not ten metres away from that spot. A month or two later, I was deep in a state of emptiness when a boy came up. You know the type: cropped hair, dull insolent expression, small intelligent eyes full of menace. "If ye're a statue, ye'll no feel this then," he said and landed me a kick in the shins with one of his heavy boots. I was vaguely conscious of the pain and the possibility that he would repeat his action, but so concentrated was I on emptiness that those thoughts wilted like weeds under a heavy sun. Later I would surmise that it was the very solidity of my essence that had deterred him from further action. That evening I returned home like a conquering hero. I felt the greatness of my achievement and then I knew that this is something I can do, for some inexplicable reason that I should never challenge. Some people, many people think we are ridiculous. At times, I have thought so too. But like any other art, you have to take it and yourself seriously – but not so seriously that you don't learn from your mistakes. I clearly had.

These are the things you must remember, if you too want to be a statue.

Stubborn passivity. In our society we don't rate passivity. It is associated with a doormat – an object that everyone tramples on and uses for scraping the dirt off their shoes. Passivity contributes nothing, or so it is thought. This is perhaps true of needy, fretful passivity that arises solely from timidity that cannot mask underlying wants, but stubborn passivity that detaches consciousness can be as influential as activism, perhaps more so. The passivity I speak of is the one that derives from having as few wants as possible, and a sense of detachment from the self.

That kind of passivity can incite, excite, stupefy and perhaps simulate an aura of holiness. It can be an act. Surely it is always an act, for where is there a soul entirely free of wants and entirely detached from the self? It is an impossibility, but I know from my own art that you can get close – or fairly close. Some might think it sad that you can only approach virtue by suppressing every part of your being. I can understand that, because once I thought like them.

My routine. I am, as you have probably guessed, a creature of predictable behaviour – a habitudinarian, some might say. I maintain the level plain of my existence by never deviating from my rigid routine of creative work and intelligent repose. You might ask where my life is going; you may wonder at the monotony of it. That is because you have not understood the purpose of existence, which is not excitement and agitation.

My working day consists of two shifts, each of three hours and fifteen minutes. They are separated by a half-hour break, which takes me to a café in Gordon Street. It is unwise to eat too much before work, but you do need a certain amount of calories for the heavy task of emptying your mind. I have one sandwich and a cappuccino.

How we can save the world. It recently occurred to me, while walking home on a pleasant summer afternoon after a particularly rewarding day lifted by my public's appreciation of my inanimate spectacle, that I was endowed with a skill which shall prove most useful to the betterment and survival of humanity. We live in a world that is overflowing with isms, as we all know: communism, capitalism, liberalism, conservatism, consumerism, materialism, imperialism, terrorism, centralism, provincialism, cosmopolitanism, intellectualism, rationalism, cyberactivism, impressionism, Dadaism, modernism, post-modernism and whatever comes after that.

And why, do you suppose, are there all these isms? Very sensibly, you haven't given it much thought. No matter, I can reveal the cause: it is the absurd human compulsion to rack one's brains, to ponder, to ruminate, and to take out that old, moth-eaten thinking cap. In other words, thought itself. And what is thought if not the destruction of our longed-for universality, because it is little else than fragmentation – the pointless fragmentation – of all things into smaller and smaller categories. Demetrius came up with atoms, which is pretty extreme and he'd never met one. That's where all that cogitation took him: the indivisible unit. It was of no use to man or beast, but it was of use to the people who like to think too much. They went off and divided the indivisible into nucleus, neutrons, protons and electrons. Were they happy with that? Of course not, they then went after quarks.

There is, of course, something extremely egotistical about the way these people put reality through the mincer. In their destructive glee on seeing our material world crumble before their prying eyes, they spare not a thought for the rest of us, who can no longer trust the ground we walk on. Nothing is solid, and everything some kind of abstraction.

Thought then is subversive. Not only does it separate and categorise, it also divides us all between the many interpretations. People go to war over ideas or over things or over competing groups. All distinctions. All animate distinctions and follies.

If, I suddenly wondered, we were all to empty our minds entirely of thoughts and become statues, how many benefits would accrue to humanity and its beloved planet? So many, so many.

There would be no thought. There would be no argument. There would be no disagreement. There would be no hatred or love. There would be no war. There would be universal harmony.

What wonder, what bounty, what glory to my name!

I encounter some contradictions in my plans and how I resolve them through a second epiphany. Once I was satisfied solely by my art and its development, but following my discovery, I became aware of the special nature of my artistic vocation and my responsibility to share it with the world. I even gave my art a name – a proper name: human concretism. One might even say that, given the importance of what I am about to reveal, my plans for humanity must be implemented, *whatever the cost* – even at the cost of my own artistic integrity, and you cannot put it stronger than that.

The problem I encountered was the one of supply. If we all become statues, then who will provide the food, the clothing and, above all, the huge quantities of theatrical makeup that will be needed if these plans are to come to fruition? Hertford University Services would not be up to the task. I imagined the city of Hertford, a dull city carefully planned by corporate architects on a limited budget. A worthy place, in a way, with a small university, public library, hospital and other public buildings all invented at the same time and in the same style that is not a style. Houses all in a row with lots of garden, as you'd expect in a country with so much land. And then in the corner of this measured utopia, there suddenly grows this industrial behemoth that is Hertford University Services. It has to send to every region of the world for the essential ingredients for make-up. Quarries, distilleries, factories, warehouses, lorries, ships, aeroplanes, railways all working flat out to turn every last inhabitant of this planet into a statue. Who would do this work? Who would slave to liberate others? Who would forego the enlightenment of nihilism, nothingness and not knowing?

Then came this second epiphany: why was I in anguish, if not because I had heard that siren call of contemplation, and given into its deceptive lure? Of course, of course, I could not defeat thought by thinking. We will bring the universe together by a revolutionary act of all becoming statues, and that act will bring about a cataclysm that will be beyond redemption and considerations of a purely practical nature.

New energies will be produced and we might easily turn into stone – we might all petrify quite literally. A world of human statues irreversibly transformed into a higher consciousness or, rather, a sophisticated lack of it.

My place within the universe. The reason I eschewed the industrial solution is that I am fundamentally an egalitarian. But the only guaranteed form of equality relies on equal subservience to a supreme leader – the helmsman, the sun about which all things must orbit, the saviour of our solidity.

Now when I wander home, I sometimes catch myself muttering aloud or another person glancing at me as though I were acting strangely. Little do they know, I think, what plans I have for them and how I can liberate them. Little do they know how soon they will know my name and thank me from the bottom of their hearts for all the changes I am bringing. Little do they know that these mutterings are the fine-tunings of a cosmic plan.

I am relaxed about the fact that it has, after all, fallen to me to engage in thought: fire must be fought with fire, and the vanguard through its sacrifice earns the right to a special morality.

Forks in the Road

"He undermined me," the husband said. "He purposefully undermined. He wanted me out of the practice, for one reason only…"

She felt the pause, and its predictability weighed on her like a leaden cape.

"… he was threatened by my greater knowledge of medical science, my skill, my brilliance."

Once he'd finished, she felt a slight relief… and the absurdity of it could not be denied. It was always a difficult moment: the union between the instability of alcohol and the instability arising from the conflicting emotions of self-belief and self-pity. And in her relief she allowed herself the flicker of a smile.

He caught it. Amidst the fog of his brain, something latched on to that millimetric quiver at the sides of her mouth, and enlarged them into something grotesque, disdainful and even threatening: laughter or even a cackle.

"Go on, laugh! Laugh, if you find me so funny," he leaned across to her and his large bloodshot eyes stared cruelly, like those of an animal, fierce and not receptive to human reason. Yet it was him, surely. Her husband, the man she'd been married to for nineteen years.

"You think you're really something, don't you?" he continued and laughed himself. She welcomed his laugh, because she knew that this situation could go two ways and the laugh meant that he was very possibly moving towards the point where he would say, "That's my gutsy little girl," and try to kiss her, which was always preferable. He stood up straight, as though to steady the thing that was spinning his head and could go either way. He was like a maddened bear, and now there was so much of him. When she first met him, he had been tall but slim with hard, muscly limbs; he had now become flabby but much, perhaps most, of his strength remained. Sodden condescension and sentimentality seemed less likely now he'd raised himself to his full height. The thing that was spinning in his brain was losing its spin, and would almost certainly go the wrong way. Her nerves tautened and her senses sharpened like a frightened beast's.

"Amazing really how much you put up with," he said slowly with a terrifying coolness. "You came along, grabbed my family name, used my contacts, clambered up above me and kicked me in the teeth."

Experience had taught her never to reply. There was no proper reply to these groundless accusations which nevertheless gained a kind of awkward authenticity through endless repetition. To deny or to mollify would only increase their currency. Her silence was watchful.

Then it came with theatrical suddenness. His left hand grabbed the kitchen table on the right side and upturned it, flinging it to the left with unnecessary force. The breakfast crockery shattered loudly on the tiled floor, while knives and spoons tinkled like muted musical instruments. In spite of her alertness, she didn't see it coming. With a single action, that same left hand returned and slapped her so violently she was thrown from her chair. He picked up the stainless-steel fruit press and threw it at her head, but she was already elsewhere with the quickness of a cat, her only advantage. Not enough though, in that confined space, to avoid his steely grip for long. This time he had her by the neck pressed up against the refrigerator. He appeared to be wanting to lift her off the floor: too much even for his strength. "I'll fucking kill you," he said, and she panicked. He had never said that before and it felt that this was how her life was going to end.

And what a miserable life. Her father, though not physically abusive, had been authoritarian and never ceased to humiliate her mother with the cruel sarcasm of a bitter man – someone who might also have complained of a miserable existence and unfulfilled hopes, not because of lack of talent but lack of opportunities. When she met her husband, her father scoffed: "Never did a hand's tap. A soft boy from a public school. You'll regret it because people like that are needy." Now she could see that her father had not been emotionally needy in the way her husband was, and she had never learned to provide for that neediness. Her father was a self-sufficient man and thus a different kind of despot, and, the worst of it, he'd been right, and thus able to smile smugly: "I told you so." Those inevitable words, cruelly repeated. The truth as another cudgel that fell on her head. She had been the first in her family to go to university and found it a liberation, but hopes of a better, freer life had proved illusory. And now this was how it would all end. Strangled or her head battered against the fridge or the wall. She was a plaything in his large podgy hands, and an object barely perceived by his sluggish consciousness. She was a liberated woman; how could she finish up like this? It was absurd and shameful.

Now it was her mind that was spinning between two possibilities: the final acceptance of an early death as a not altogether uninviting destiny, or the absolute struggle to free herself from that unjust fate by whatever means. The first was the languid desire for release that comes from a tiredness accumulated over nearly two decades of hard work at home and at the law firm where she was a senior partner, and the second came from an instinct so deep within our psyches that it pushes all aside – the will to live that comes most fiercely in the moments of fiercest danger. The will to live has no rational basis; it springs from our animal nature but it does not last. It is all instinct and all moment, and when it comes, time itself seems to slow down.

The knife-block was on the work surface just next to the fridge, and her hand quickly grasped the first handle she could find. Fortunately the blade was short, and in a second it was in his gut.

His expression switched immediately to one of surprise and disbelief, quickly followed by terror. It partially sobered him up and he detached himself to wander clumsily around the kitchen, noisily kicking or stamping on the various items he'd thrown or tipped on to the floor. "The little whore has killed me," he said, as though there were someone else in the room, "that's women for you. No loyalty, no gratitude."

When she studied him in his hospital bed, she found it very difficult to feel sorry for him, although he made up for that by feeling very sorry for himself. He looked absurd. Like the giant who fell from the beanstalk, but with less right to complain, she thought. Nevertheless, he did, although he interspersed his lamentations with pleas for her understanding. "Don't leave me. I couldn't manage without you. This may seem strange, but I couldn't live without you and it has not been easy for me to admit that. I shouldn't have hit you; I know that now. But then again, you shouldn't provoke me. I'm not someone to provoke, you know," he said simply.

But the simplicity didn't work. He revolted her. Dear God, did life have to be this difficult, she thought, though she was not a religious woman. Indeed her values very much reflected her own times, so how come she had ended up in a situation that belonged to a different age? He was, she told herself endlessly, the father of their son who'd been killed in a hit-and-run incident at the age of eleven. He'd been abusive before that, but the death of his child had made things worse. Was he also a victim? In that moment, she thought not.

He had not been a good father. Detached and ambitious at the time, he seemed hardly to notice the boy, but no doubt his son was an important part of his identity. Dealing with her husband's pain had distracted her from her own. That was a kind of balm. But then again she failed there too. He started to drink heavily and eventually lost his job. There had always been something theatrical about her husband: his booming voice in a slightly exaggerated upper-class accent, his flamboyant dress, his long, Oscar Wilde locks and, most of all, his absolute belief in the importance of what he had to say. He projected himself onto others as though they were a screen – an inanimate object that served to reflect his glorious self. This character might be defined as Churchillian, but somewhere along the thread of his life it took a different turn: it lacked the public element of the statesman, which might mean that at least he didn't suffer from megalomania or might mean, more simply, that his horizons were more limited. Beneath the bluff exterior, some detected a weakness, a terror, a lack of self-belief rather than a surfeit. She often thought that, and it was the only thing she loved about him. Her love then was based on a doubtful hypothesis, as she well knew. The precision of her analysis did not help her to make sensible decisions.

A policeman had come round to tell her that they would not be pressing charges. He explained that her husband had been insistent on dropping the case, but the police could still have proceeded. Given, however, her husband's insistence and his repeated claim that the marriage could survive the violent encounter, the procurator fiscal had decided to drop the case. "But it was self-defence," she said, struggling to understand. The policeman stared at her, as though having his own difficulty with that inability of hers. "The knife was embedded in two inches of flesh; a thinner man might have died," he explained with no reference to her own point, which, thus dismissed, appeared to have no relevance. That was the first she'd heard of her husband's desire to continue the relationship. It disappointed her. She thought that the events of that evening must mean the end of that phase of her life. He too disappointed her once more, as his behaviour showed a lack of dignity. But surely she had shown a lack of dignity by remaining all those years with a violent husband until eventually she had felt obliged to react. Violence degrades both perpetrator and victim, but in different ways. Or that was what she felt. She also felt that leaving home was not a particularly attractive proposition, especially now she knew that he would be forever pestering her to come back, using moral blackmail and evoking their dead son.

Had she been present when her husband was visited by his drinking pal, Bill, she would have had no difficulty in deciding what to do. After all, she earned a good salary and could quite easily start again. Many women in her situation did not share that luxury.

Bill had lost his job about the same time as her husband did. They simply made him redundant along with a thousand other workers at the plant producing sanitary goods for public toilets. Her husband had avoided dismissal for years: he was listened to sympathetically and the practice even hired a psychologist. He was given compassionate leave, and then given it again and again. In the end it was his erratic and violent behaviour towards patients that finally convinced his employers that they had to let him go. Still he did entertain the possibility of taking them to a tribunal, but after some research his lawyer decided that, on balance, it would be better not to. Bill was given the minimum of everything: a pitiful redundancy payment based on a pitiful salary, a few weeks' notice and a written request for the return of his company-issue work jacket. Alcohol took Bill in a different direction. He was at last able to give free rein to his fecklessness. After six months, his wife had had enough and she showed him the door. Always a mild-mannered man, he dutifully left without a scene. He was supposed to take the children out once a week, but it was more like once a month. He wanted to be a good father, but he always wanted to be a good father next month. This month, he had to drink, as though it were a duty, a job, even an imposition.

Bill and her husband were an unlikely pair. The latter liked to play the bounteous friend to the only person left he could talk down to. Bill on the other hand thought that he had found a lost soul badly in need of a helping hand, and he was closer to the truth, although he did have one ulterior motive: an endless succession of free drinks, which she probably paid for.

"The little whore nearly killed me," he said, quoting himself, "that's women for you. No loyalty, no gratitude." Bill nodded, but disagreed. He knew his friend had a violent temper, and he knew his wife was a petite and attractive woman, whose attractiveness was not sexual or aesthetic so much as decency enclosed within a

gaunt and noble exterior. She was as energetic as they were lacka-
daisical. It hurt him therefore that she clearly considered him to
be part of the problem – to be leading her husband astray. "We're
both looking after him," he wanted to say, "and I'm keeping him
out of your road." But of course he didn't. In fact he didn't say anything to her, and on the few occasions they met, it was because his
friend had forced him to come back to the house, clearly against
her own wishes.

Seonag came round with the obligatory bottle of red wine. "It's
time you listened to your friends. This can't go on," she said with
proprietorial kindness.

But she, the woman apparently in need of friends, didn't feel
she needed them. Her life was not so good that it merited raking
over. Besides, she had always slightly envied Seonag's good luck
in life: widely admired, she had children and a doting husband, a
little dull perhaps and a new man – possibly. Seonag would have
wanted a dull husband anyway; she had to shine. Seonag wasn't
even that good to look at, she thought rather basely. An unsist-
erly thought she was supposed to have placed in the dustbin of
history, which would be overflowing if it weren't for the fact that
everything you throw in it immediately leaps out again. Things
were bad, and the last thing she needed was Seonag telling her
how to live her life. They sat in the sitting room – a lacklus-
tre and featureless expression of a marriage so troubled it could
never express anything except a void. Seonag made a great play
of pouring the wine to emphasise her feisty and upbeat role in her
friend's crisis. "You've got to leave, you must know that. What
you're doing visiting him in hospital, I can't imagine." Seonag
allowed herself a momentary glance of disapproval in her direction, but she didn't react to Seonag's prodding. She wasn't going
to answer, partly because she hadn't made up her mind – something she was ashamed of. It's not that simple, she thought, but
didn't say. She knew what Seonag's reply would be, "But it is that
simple. It's cut and dried. The man is off his head. What is it with
women who always think they can reform their men, even after

decades of absolute proof to the contrary?" Unlike her forename, Seonag's surname and Seonag's accent did not betray a Gaelic background; her wealthy parents had chosen Gaelic names for their children as a nod towards their nationalist instincts. She had been educated at a private academy and her genuinely well-meaning campaigns were often invasive, as they failed to take account of their beneficiaries' subjectivity. There was something a little faux about Seonag: she seemed to be made up of disparate elements that she had laboriously welded together to construct a self that might or might not have worked, but certainly acted as a veil to her true nature; she seemed to be the archetypal product of a fragmented age, and that too must have required a degree of courage on her part.

Her petite friend was not unappreciative, but she needed time to think and was perfectly aware of the arguments. She sipped her wine and said little. This only made Seonag say more, and by the time she left, her friend was almost convinced that she had to stay with her husband. Life didn't seem to offer much else, and the world outside her ghastly marriage seemed to be populated by the judgmental.

The hospital rang in the morning. It was a chirpy young nurse who clearly didn't know the background to the case. "Mrs ...," she said; it was "Mrs" and not "Ms" as though to emphasise the bond. "Mrs ... the consultant says your husband can come home this afternoon. Any time after three. Is that all right?"

She said nothing. She could not reply.

"Mrs ..., are you all right?" the nurse said nervously.

"I'm fine. That'll be fine," she said flatly, unthinkingly. "I'll be there to take him home."

She had hoped for more time, even though she knew she would never resolve the problem. As long as he was away, the thoughts would just keep spinning around in her head. Spinning and spinning. Interrupting her work, distracting her and wearing down her already threadbare nerves. What she feared most was not his violence – that would come later – but the theatrical scene with which he would greet her. Exactly what form it would take was hard to say. What was certain was that he would write his part well and extract the maximum pathos. He would be the Christ whose flesh had been torn; he would be the magnanimous husband who receives his penitent wife. She would turn red with shame, speechless and unable to defend herself for fear of aggravating the excruciating spectacle. Always that threat hanging over her, but could she live without it now? The last nineteen years of her life had been marked by the continuous presence of that threat. It had become an integral part of life; how would she fare without it? And what about him? He really did need her, she knew that. Even if he was capable of killing her – of that she was now certain – death in the sadness and ugliness of her life did not seem so terrible. They shared a lot, man and wife, and what they shared was a past she was not sure she could ever be free of. He too was a soul in pain. The strong have to suffer for the weak, and she was strong enough to carry him through life. On his own, he would not go far. She would have no more children, so he was the only person in absolute need of her sacrifice. Hadn't he promised never to hit her again? If he kept that promise, surely everything was bearable – but only bearable.

As the afternoon progressed, she became increasingly convinced that to abandon a human being with whom she had jointly suffered and delighted in so much was wrong. Not only were there those moments of strife, but also those to be relished: the birth of their son, family holidays abroad, encounters with friends, and yes, love, especially in the early years. Was it not childish to think that life is like an advert – a continuous thread of unalloyed joy? True, her love was long dead, and his physical touch revolted her, but her compassion for him was not entirely extinguished. Emotions are not like rational concepts: the contradictory can cohabit very easily.

She opened her umbrella and ran to the car. The drab weather of the west coast clung to everything. The sodden ground shifted under her tread and her bones felt the sharpness of the wind. We are born into an alien world whose trials would make the immortal gods weep, if they had any compassion; yet we must bear them in solitude precisely because we are not alone. Indeed she was lucky when compared with so much of humanity and of womankind – she had, some might say, little to complain about in a world of smart bombs, sweatshops, sex slaves, people-trafficking, famine and brutal, unremitting physical labour that does not earn a living wage. To feel sorry for oneself is to lose that last shred of human dignity. She straightened her secular Presbyterian back, and decided she was definitely going to the hospital.

Just before a T-junction she pulled into a lay-by and took a deep breath. This needed more thought, she told herself. Once we pretend to be returning to normality, it will be so much harder to break free, and this is someone I have stabbed. For the first time, she felt the enormity of having almost killed someone. Why put herself in a position where that same dynamic of violent attack and violent defence could repeat itself?

She also rebelled against the way others would inevitably interpret their continued marriage: "Of course, it was six of one and half a dozen of the other." She could also hear people say, "You can hardly blame him, she's as dull as ditchwater." It was true, she thought, she was a little dull, as so many overworked and reliable people are. The ebullient couthieness so valued in our society had been drained out of her long ago. But surely, where there is violence, all blame must be with the perpetrator. Absolute rules are dangerous, but this one must stand. It is not even three of one and nine of the other; it is all blame on one side. And yet there could be no doubt, she had always felt more diminished by his violence than he did. Perhaps he didn't feel diminished at all.

The now heavy rain flooded the windscreen, isolating her in the car interior that felt like the whole universe. She was alone in it, with only her pain for company. She turned the ignition far enough to restart the wipers, and they revealed a monochrome drabness in which the junction and its choices could only just be discerned. The two directions – left towards the hospital or right towards Seonag's comfortable detached villa and a different kind of humiliation. Outside the car was a world so strange and unnatural that she couldn't feel part of it. Others in her situation might have been tempted by suicide, but she, still a practical and resourceful woman in spite of her suffering, wrestled with a deep sense of alienation like someone unsettled by a particularly obscure cryptic crossword puzzle.

Did it make sense to climb into bed or even share a house with someone who at one level repelled her? If love means anything at all, it is not eventually about a loved one's looks. If he were like Adonis or even his youthful self, he would still repel her, just as a kindlier, more admirable or more fascinating man would have retained her love even if he had grown into her husband's current appearance. Love that endures is not only proximity and habituation; it is also a unique culture, a system of communication, a world view, a sense of humour and, in its highest form, a complete lack of possession. Their marriage lacked all those things. Better to be alone, much better.

She switched the ignition off so that the rainwater could obscure the dullness and unattractiveness of her choices.

But wasn't most of her rejection of Seonag's kind offer just pride? Was she rejecting it, simply because it was so unfamiliar: an unknown bedroom and outside it the sense of intruding in the privacy of other lives, the exaggerated attentiveness of Seonag's husband, the exuberance of their children, and the bitter taste of other people's food day after day? But not forever.

She could go to a hotel. She was not poor, although the cost would soon clock up. Practical as she was, she knew that she wouldn't resist him if he turned up at the hotel. She hated scenes in public places. If he came to Seonag's, Seonag would send him packing. Seonag was good at that kind of thing. He would scream and plead and threaten, and Seonag would stand her ground, while she would sit in her bedroom in anguish, embarrassed that her friend was fighting her battles. But it would not go on indefinitely.

She switched the engine on, pulled out of the lay-by, reached the T-junction and swung to the right, as though it were just one motion. "The bastard can take the bus," she muttered to herself.

And so she reached the end of all those forks in the road. Decisions still had to be made, but none so crucial as that series of difficult choices between unpalatable opposites that opened up entirely different lives. And up and down the country, many others faced similar choices and still do. Many not so lucky or so determined once the choice was made.

In That Moment

In that moment, he was running. The balls of his feet were pounding so hard on the tarmac, they began to hurt. His heart was a frightened animal leaping in the cage of his chest. He was aware of that sinewy pump accelerating as it fuelled on adrenalin. Fit to burst. To break. To let him down. Why? Why was he here? Frightened. Gasping for breath. Why here? Giancarlo del Padrone. Thief. Petty thief. Father. Father to three kids. Short prison terms. Misdemeanours. Always just a couple of weeks. The careless slips. Slips that poor men make. Now he's dead. Shot on the roof. Shot for a protest. What about? More time in the exercise yard. So little surely? *Keep running. Don't think. The jeep's just behind you.* So little to concede. Exercise. Try this for exercise. Too much. Exercise. Too much. Fit to burst. And fear. Such fear he'd never known. His heart. Giancarlo. Del Padrone. Padrone. Del. Del. Del. Run. Run. Run. Stop! *The jeep has turned off in pursuit of others. Catch your breath and relax. You've made it, have you not?* He stopped and drank in the air in great, unmannerly gulps. He bent double and his legs turned to jelly. He rested his hands on his bent knees, and continued to gasp at the air like an animal in the wrong element. But he laughed, glad to have avoided a beating. He'd done his bit and he'd made it. And then the laughter drained from him, as he became aware of the risk he'd run and pictured his bleeding body on the cobbles. They could have broken arms or, worse, his head. For what? Did he think he could bring Del Padrone back to life? Did he think he could make a difference in a game in which only his kind pays any price? Would Del Padrone's widow get better compensation if they cracked his head?

Then he heard it – another police jeep rounding a corner,

screeching metallic anger. He had to run. He turned and saw two grim, humourless faces – their concentrated expression betrayed another harsh reality as terrifying as the machine they drove; these men were well practised in what they did. More training meant less humanity. More training meant that man and machine were more fully fused into a whole – metal and flesh were now of one substance. One policeman was grossly overweight and the other slim and bronzed. One to catch him and one to break his ribs with a boot whose persuasiveness came from a hundred and twenty kilos of fat. Others were already running, panicked like sheep, but his muscles were loose, failed to harden and spring. The jeep sounded its horn and urgency once more took hold. Those hamstrings started to pull, his heart began to beat. Right or left? Left or right, or go straight on for another block? Was it best to go with the crowd or for him to be alone or with one or two?

Take the right, take the right and stay with the melee. He turned at a fast jog and saw with a quickness he didn't think he had that three policemen were giving a young girl a good three weeks in hospital. The left, the left, it should have been the left. Panicked, he turned again and no longer sought safety in numbers. The road he took was empty. An abandoned newspaper kiosk had been hurriedly closed and the billboard announced the "tragic death" of Giancarlo del Padrone, father of three, and showed his mother's weeping face. An accidental death, they said. The public should await the investigating magistrate's report. He allowed his feet to stop running but forced them still to walk.

They had shot not once, but several times to terrify the prisoners into submission. The neighbourhood was restless...

The prison roof was not just any roof; it was just three blocks up the road where he lived. He knew Del Padrone vaguely and had been at school with his younger brother. What did "Del Padrone" mean, if not that one of their ancestors had been the illegitimate child of his mother's boss or landowner – the kind of person who doesn't belong to either class and is rejected by the church. He knew Del Padrone and he perceived the prisoner's death as an attack on his world, his part of the city. He was not alone in this:

during the riot, old ladies had handed down slices of lemon and orange to counter the effects of teargas.

Don't stop. Don't relax. He had slowed to a saunter along the pavement, deep in thought and certain that now he was simply a citizen walking the streets of his city. Then another jeep came round the corner; it was the same one, circling around in search of quarry increasingly difficult to find as the demonstrators dispersed. He turned and recognised the two policemen, one fat and one thin – an odd couple despite their professional verve. He froze and saw the jeep ride up on the pavement without breaking its speed. He had time enough to see his killers, a luxury Del Padrone had not enjoyed. He noted the blankness of their expressions, although there was perhaps a hint of contrary emotions, as though they were already inventing their vindication while savouring a moment of heightened existence through violence.

The impact was sudden and devastating. He was lifted off his feet and projected in space, while the driver hit the brakes. He might have survived had he not collided with the metal pillar of a road sign. He bounced off and fell close to the pavement: it appeared that he was already dead. The fat man lifted himself out of the jeep slowly and purposefully, with the air of someone who has been distracted from more important things.

"*Che bello spintone gli hai dato!* That was a nice little shove you gave him!" the thin man said as he sat immobile and apparently a little bored. After his inspection, which included a quick look at the front of the jeep, the fat man went over to his colleague and said more quietly, "He's dead." They both adopted a look of insolent defensiveness – perhaps the expression Giancarlo del Padrone wore when he appeared before the magistrate, but not likely. More likely would be that he was apprehensive in court and intimidated by the trappings of authority. Surely he was more anxious over his misdemeanour than these men were over a killing, but rightly so: the policemen acted with a wide, albeit not boundless, margin of impunity. They immediately set about a few precautions. The thin man moved the jeep off the pavement and parked it a metre in front of the cadaver. Of course nothing would add up, if there were a thorough investigation. The fat man walked up and down the street, looking to both sides. He noticed an old woman's face in the window, but did not see her for long enough to register her features. He went over to the entrance to the flats and made a mental note of the number. He returned to the jeep, by which time the thin man was looking peeved. After all, he hadn't been driving at the time. They then stood by their vehicle and waited for the authorities to come and investigate the authorities.

His body lay twisted in a small amount of his own blood, a victim of his own compassion, a symbol of the heroism of mortals, or perhaps the randomness of human lives, just as pebbles lie in a stream and slip over each other, making their erratic way down a hill's irresistible declivity.

The Selfish Geneticist

Dick Chomley is the energetic purveyor of a threadbare philosophy, which has the merit of reassuring the spirit of our conformist times. Every now and then we citizens of mature democracies who benefit from a high standard of living, good education and utterly free and reliable news media, wake up and have this scary moment of doubt: Are we selfish? Do we need all this stuff? Do we know what's going on? Are we perhaps less skilled than our forebears? And, most distressingly, is there any point to this life? At this stage, our perfectly balanced market economies provide us the necessary balm: the Panglossian works of Professor Dick Chomley – *Egotism is Nature*, *Anything You Do Is DNA-Driven*, *Religion is a Madness* and *God Got Lost on the Way to the Toilet*, all translated into every one of our European languages and many more besides.

He is very prolific but does everything he can to prove his theories wrong. Instead of desperately pursuing his instinctive urge to procreate, he spends most of his time closed up in his study – like a monk in his cell – writing the same book with a different title in the company of two busts, one of Voltaire and one of Einstein. Now you and I, who don't have a grounding in modern philosophical thought and its various subtleties, think that Voltaire and Einstein were very intelligent men, but Chomley has demonstrated beyond all reasonable doubt that they weren't that clever, because they said they were Deists, when they really meant to say atheists. Nor does it occur to our dear Panglossian philosopher during his tirades against religions that, if Voltaire believed in anything, he believed in the absolute tolerance of other people's religious views.

But of course we are talking of a higher truth here, and the higher truth is a scientific one, even when science has absolutely nothing to say on the matter. The history of life is the history of the perfect mechanism of self-interest, and while we might have some sympathy for the deification of Chaos, who previously had a rotten press, are we happy with the deification of Over-Simplification?

Some might find Chomley's professional life and routine a little dull, but he always appears to be a little excited and desperate to proselytise. His lecture at Oxford University a few months ago was quite typical of his work, but it furnished the opportunity for him to rekindle his acquaintance with Lord Hexham, the remarkable geneticist who studied under Crick and Watson and did so much to establish Britain's leading role in the field. He continued their work and became something of a populariser during the New Labour years: hence the peerage. This is good for you the reader, and for me: on his own Chomley would provide little entertainment.

There they were: the serried ranks of the *fior fiore* of British academe, well dressed much as the middle classes were when they went to church in the nineteenth century. Suits were worn, dresses were long, noses were lifted, smiles were well exercised, voices were exuberant, or, to put it in our modern tongue, there was a buzz about the place. Not, I should add, because anyone expected anything original to be said; this was one of those opera houses where the audience is more important than the opera.

Someone very important came on the platform to introduce the speaker. He looked like a boy on his birthday, which must have been exhausting; this effusion is now *de rigueur* – today, tomorrow and the bloody next day. Whatever happened to old-fashioned English grumpiness? "Your speaker, who is now a household name, is perhaps the academic I most admire in the world," he said, which left open the possibility of rivals on other planets in our solar system. To be fair, he didn't use this accolade before every lecture he introduced but he had used it five times in the previous twelve months. "There are several reasons for this: the thoroughness of his research, the impartiality of his analysis, the exquisiteness of his prose, the generosity of his spirit; but, ladies and gentlemen, fellow scientists and fellow academics, surely it is his intellectual integrity that most impresses us." The applause was rapturous. People discreetly looked around to assess the enthusiasm of the audience, and more than one heart was touched by the silliest of all emotions: envy. "I have known Dick for many years – long before his rise to fame – and I can say without fear of contradiction that his good nature remains entirely unspoilt by success. You see, what's special about Dick is that he is completely unaware of how much influence he has on the intellectual life of Britain today. I could go on but I won't, because Dick is quite capable of speaking up for himself. So without further ado, I hand you over to Dick Chomley!"

At that moment, Chomley walked on, nonchalantly grinning at the very important man. They both embraced like old friends who had not seen each other in years, while in fact the same scene had been played out not an hour beforehand in the very important man's spacious study and followed by fine wines and hors d'oeuvres in the company of the *fior fiore* of the *fior fiore*.

Chomley then walked to the lectern. He reverently placed his heavy tome of Darwin's *Collected Works* on it, and opened the work at the first coloured marker. He looked up, catching the light from the stained-glass windows of the old university. He stared fixedly as though gathering his energies for an onerous but unavoidable task, and then started to read in a slightly monotonous tone. The lesson for the day was from *The Descent of Man and Selection in Relation to Sex*:

"Darwin was quite specific about evolution within the human species, and I think we should be bold enough to take note of this. We live in a highly civilised era and sometimes we are overly sensitive about some issues. This is what he wrote, 'Nor is the difference slight in moral disposition between a barbarian, such as the man described by the old navigator Byron, who dashed his child on the rocks for dropping his basket of sea-urchins, and a Howard or a Clarkson; and in intellect, between a savage who uses hardly any abstract terms, and a Newton or Shakespeare. Differences of this kind between the highest of men of the highest races and the lowest savages, are connected to the finest gradations. Therefore it is possible that they might pass and be developed into each other.'

"Clearly we are an evolving species and we need to help those who are not the 'highest of men' and are not from the 'highest races', although we would prefer to put it less starkly: 'those whose cerebral functions are not so highly developed' and 'those whose ethnic DNA types present some limitations'. In other words, we have to have concern for the genetic health of our populations."

Some of those whose cerebral functions were highly developed were finding it difficult to follow Chomley's argument. One man scratched his thigh vigorously. A prim lady with round glasses coughed as she tried to follow the journey of a ladybird around the velvety collar of the man sitting in front; was there a point to all this expenditure of energy? she asked herself. A stout and jowly man kept slipping into the most pleasurable sleep and subsequently snoring, while his wife used the sharpness of her elbow to wake him temporarily. A serious-minded scientist who had pumped Chomley's hand vigorously and repeatedly when they met over the fine wines and hors d'oeuvres could not keep his eyes off the clock. A young, obese woman was fidgeting in spite of her cumbersome frame, because she felt sure that she had detected a significant flaw in the great man's argument. The immensity of this truth was agitating her and she wanted to communicate it immediately to everyone else in the room and indeed to all humanity. Various other manifestations of restlessness and inattention were occurring around the room, but the speaker seemed unaware as he leapt erratically from one obsession to another. Sometimes there seemed to be little connection between them, but everything he said led to one great truth: we are all perfectly made machines that are constantly evolving and designed not by God but by survival of the fittest, or rather we are constructed by the perfectly made machine of natural selection, which surely must be one of our new gods.

Perhaps amongst that crowd of well-protected and, some might say, highly pampered genes with good chances of selection as their bodies warmed the cold and ancient stones that, over the centuries, had heard all manner of fashionable truths, whilst the faces of the speakers never seemed to change, there lurked a murderer, but I doubt he had a murderous face. The man in the tweed jacket and designer glasses, with an air of studied nonchalance, the academic smile of knowing appreciation and the stare of utter absorption in the arguments expounded by Dick Chomley, was probably thinking about his lover or whether he could keep up with the mortgage payments. He played the part too well. So what could natural selection do with this lot? It no doubt worked quite well, when we were all hunter-gatherers or when we were our missing ancestors, competing in the same way within the same environment, but now? It would require omniscience to understand this wonderful, talented and idiotic jumble of humanity. We need a little more than is dreamed of in your philosophy, Dick Chomley.

"Michelangelo may well have been a Christian – there wasn't really any choice at the time – but his Christianity did not create his art." Dick Chomley must use the same history consultants as Hollywood: Michelangelo was not only a Christian, but one of the fanatical "Spirituals" who caught the attention of the Inquisition. Some felt that his art reflected his heretical views. But if Christianity, according to Chomley, can take no credit for Western civilisation, it seems a bit unfair for him to argue that those great works of art the Church didn't commission would have been ruined by their commissioning of it.

He furthered his attack on the monotheist religions by quoting particularly bellicose adherents from each one; the more peace-loving and just loving examples were not referred to. He ended his speech with a fine example of his sophisticated rhetoric: he invited deluded believers everywhere "to dream on".

As soon as that injunction was made to no one in that room, because it was directed at the stupid who live elsewhere, the very important man returned to the platform, hugged Dick Chomley again and, turning to the audience, lifted Chomley's hand in the air as though he were a prize-fighter. And the prize-fighter was ecstatic. Ecstasy, however, did not cloud his intellect; even as the applause lifted him on a wave of joy, he scanned the crowd for faces he might know. He found them, but his vision leapt on past them: he wasn't fishing for tadpoles. Then he saw Lord Hexham and immediately he left the platform and pushed his way through the pressing throng, one part of which was heading towards him loud with congratulations while the other part was heading for the exit. Regrettably Lord Hexham was in the second category. Clearly he would have to be a little rude if he were to catch up with his prey. "Thank you, thank you, I'm in a bit of a rush, I'm afraid." An elderly woman with a sad and reflective expression was gushing her praise: it appeared that she was no longer afraid of death after having heard his lecture. He never grasped the content of her words but pushed her gently aside, while nodding his regrets. Fortunately she took no exception to the idea that this modern thinker had no time for her; that seemed entirely understandable to her, even proper. As a pilgrim might stare at a holy man, she rapturously focused on his back whilst he struggled with the scrum.

Lord Hexham was already in the car park when Chomley caught up with him, a little out of breath and suddenly a little embarrassed in his lordship's presence. "Lord Hexham, James," he puffed, "you must excuse me, but I didn't want to let you go without having a word. So good of you to come."

Hexham, who was already stooping to get into his car, straightened up and examined the speaker he'd been listening to for an hour, as though he didn't know him.

"So very good of you to come. Really," stammered the ex-prize-fighter.

"Chomley," Hexham smiled, now the hierarchy of their relationship had been established, "good speech."

"Really?" asked Chomley brightly. "So good of you to say so. You know how much I value your opinion. I couldn't believe it when I saw you. I just had to speak to you." He didn't appear to have finished, but he had run out of words.

"Chomley, what can I do for you?" said the other.

"Well, why don't we go for a meal?"

"Hasn't the rector organised something for you?"

"Oh yes, there is an official dinner," Chomley said grandly. "But I'd prefer to have lunch with you. I know a really good restaurant."

If Hexham was flattered, he showed no sign of it. "Well, I don't see why not."

"Oh James, that's very good of you. I know you're such a busy man."

"Yes, so it'll have to be a short one."

"Of course."

As soon as the two men had sat down in the restaurant and ordered their meal, Chomley was keen to start. He was like a student at his viva, only he was asking the questions to impress rather than answering them. "So what do think of this business about building another university chapel? You'd think there were enough of them already."

Hexham looked uninterested and sipped his wine. "Just nonsense," he said eventually.

"And how about these people who say that there's no conflict between science and religion?"

"Do they?"

"Yes, you know. Science tells us who we are and religion tells us what we're for. That kind of rubbish."

"Exactly. Rubbish. Why should we be for anything? We're the products of evolution – or in other words, the products of our own desires. At this very moment, I'm *for* a damn good meal."

Chomley laughed too much, while Hexham ignored him and sipped his wine like a man who has just delivered the final word on a subject.

"A damn good meal" – well, that sums up very well what life is for in the cruder forms of materialist philosophy. The trouble with the scientific approach is that it's right about the material world, but dumb when it comes to the areas it cannot deal with, particularly the riddle of consciousness, the "ghost in the machine": intellectual conversations between Hexham and Chomley never get past guffawing and caricature.

There was silence for a bit and then Hexham said, "Got any children, Chomley?"

"No, I'm not married," came the reply. Chomley had a curiously dated sexual morality for a modern man – almost that of a fifties vicar.

"Come come, Chomley, think about your genes."

Chomley was not enjoying the conversation: "Never met the right woman, I suppose."

"Children, not all they're cracked up to be," said the lord. "The instinct might be good for the species, but they're a pain in the arse when it comes to bringing them up."

"James, I'm sure you don't mean that." Chomley, on the other hand, knew very well that Hexham had an only son of twenty-two who had just graduated at Oxford with a first-class degree in modern languages – French, Russian and Arabic.

"My son," Lord Hexham said, while fighting with a slice of beef that would not yield, "is such a fool. He could have taken his Arabic studies further for his Ph.D. It's a growth industry, I told him – anti-terrorism studies and all that. You'll get the ear of the powerful. You'll get rich. Do you know what he said?"

"It's terrible that youth won't listen. We were the same, I suppose," Dick glowed at his own modesty and self-knowledge. "What did he say?"

"He said he liked the idea of Arabic – but only to investigate the works of some thirteenth-century Sufi poet nobody has ever heard of; unfortunately his great love was Pushkin and he was determined to do a Ph.D. on some of his minor works."

"No chance of anti-terrorism studies there," Chomley smiled, "no peaceful career in the diplomatic service. What a waste of talent, eh? Bad luck, we all have to put up with a bit of that. He might come right later."

"Pushkin was part negro," Lord Hexham said, as though this was relevant.

Chomley, who was a little more politically correct, blushed and momentarily lost his smile. "The liberal establishment," he started off on another tack, "are to blame; they have always oversold the arts and humanities, while belittling the scientific community. That's why your son didn't know where to take his linguistic talents."

Lord Hexham looked at him blankly, and he was not a man to be sidetracked by dull and specious arguments. "Of course, he's a deviant anyway."

Chomley froze and wondered if anyone could overhear. "Deviant?" he whispered.

"Yes, deviant," Lord Hexham boomed. "Homosexual, queer… as bent as a nine-bob note… or whatever you want to call it."

Chomley was now very uncomfortable. "I didn't know your son was gay."

"Gay? Gay? There's nothing particularly gay about being a nancy-boy."

Chomley looked around in terror. This was a smart restaurant in Oxford, not a gentleman's club. Hexham had never had a sense of place or decorum. Was there a gene for decorum? Even though his lordship was renowned for being outspoken, Chomley decided to take a stand. But he did so hesitantly, because he valued the lord's friendship and the doors it could open – not to mention the fearsome aggression the man exuded quite naturally, as though his genes had been modified by those of a rhinoceros. "Nowadays, we don't …"

"Nowadays," Hexham roared, "nowadays? I don't care a damn about nowadays. Science hasn't got anything to do with passing fads. Christ, man, you're all theory and no practice. Aren't you the one banging on about how we need to pass on our genes? That's the motivation of all we do. Well, not much chance of that in the case of my *gay* son. And he didn't get it from me, I can tell you that. My wife is – always was – a little androgynous, you know. Not her fault, and she always supported me in everything, so I don't criticise her too much."

"Quite right," said Chomley stupidly – suffering for his stupidity the moment it spilt out.

"Of course," his lordship continued unperturbed, the idea his conversation could cause offence never having occurred to him, "I do have a son who'll continue the paternal line." He paused to smile, revealing the importance this fact held within his mind.

"Another son?"

"Yes, yes," Hexham seemed to awaken from a pleasant reverie, "wrong side of the blanket, you know."

Chomley didn't. In part he was flattered that his lordship wanted to open up, and in part he was terrified by the insaneness of his fellow diner's stream of consciousness. "Really," he stammered.

"Yes," Hexham seemed to be speaking to no one in particular, "he lives on what can only be called a sink estate – with his mother, a hellish woman who has poisoned the boy against me. For Christ's sake, I forked out enough money over the years – enough to buy a second home somewhere, but they just stay put and piss it against the wall. The money was supposed to keep her quiet, but then she turned up at our door two months ago, screaming and shouting."

"Life is quite complicated," said Chomley in the manner of a child who has just been told that Father Christmas doesn't exist.

"Bloody right! At least my one is – can't speak for anyone else."

"I'm so sorry to hear this, Jim," Chomley adopted a quiet confidential tone and daringly shifted from "James" to the more familiar "Jim".

"I don't want your pity, Chomley," his lordship retorted irritably.

Chomley was beginning to regret pursuing Hexham across the car park in order to buy him lunch, when a sumptuous lunch was offered him by the university authorities where he would have been the guest of honour. He might also have asked himself why he did it, and the answer is far from obvious: about as imponderable as the existence of God, for which the arguments against each of the opposing hypotheses are equally strong, and arguments for each of them equally weak. Actually not quite as imponderable as that, but still imponderable. Why would a man abandon comfort and praise to seek the company of a man who treats him with disdain? He certainly got no financial gain out of this transaction, quite the opposite. He had foregone good food someone else paid for to get good food for which he would have to pay all his royalties from a small Latin-American country. Was he in love with Hexham or at least sexually attracted to him? Now I know that many of us believe that ultimately all our actions are governed by sex, though not necessarily reproductive sex – enjoyable sex with the least chance of reproduction, whatever the biological drives. I don't really know what Chomley's sexual proclivities are.

What do you mean, that's not good enough? You feel you really ought to know? What is this modern obsession with knowing what people get up to in bed? Clearly you, dear reader, are one of those who believe that sex trumps everything else.

Well I would tell you, if it sounded at all interesting, but, it seems, Chomley's sexual drive is so weak that even the omniscient narrator cannot detect it. Suffice it to say that it does not appear to be the motivation that sent him rushing madly out of the lecture hall to collar his lordship. Did he do it because he wanted the man's assistance to further his career? Surely not. His career is made, and there are many others perfectly willing to assist him further. Success breeds success, almost by itself, and does not require Chomley's erratic behaviour to sustain it.

We're almost convinced that Chomley's behaviour is not based on any motivation at all, and that makes him appear endearingly eccentric. We love an eccentric precisely because eccentrics undermine the kind of arguments put forward by people like Chomley. There remains however one final doubt: what if Chomley pursues Hexham, because Hexham disdains him and does so with a certain panache that Chomley cannot accept. Chomley is intelligent enough to see that there is no evidence that Hexham will change his ways, and that very probably Hexham treats absolutely everybody with the same disdain. There is nothing rational about Chomley's behaviour, and the trigger may well reside in his unconscious, but I think we can now put our finger on it. For Chomley, Hexham is a challenge, and human beings love a challenge, which is odd because it almost always involves putting our lives and therefore our sexual organs at some small or great risk. Chomley's behaviour towards Hexham is therefore further evidence against Chomley's own arguments. Did I say that Hexham might well treat everyone with the same contempt?

A tall man in a fashionable suit was walking briskly through the restaurant, and his handsome, youthful face was betrayed by some slight greying around the temples. He had a strong muscular build, but nothing excessive: the kind of build that can be inherited but not acquired by endless workouts in the gym. Some would define the look as patrician, but his father was a miner and his mother worked for the union. There was no aggression in his movement, and there was an attractive stillness about his personality.

"Well, well," said Lord Hexham, as the man was passing their table, "the liberal establishment disdains even to acknowledge our existence."

The man turned and smiled: "Oh Jimmy, I never saw you there. How are you doing? It's a long time since I saw you last. Everything okay, I hope."

The man was about to go, but Hexham wouldn't let him: "Come, come, Johnny, you said it was a long time. Chomley here has chosen a damn good wine; pull up a chair!" And then as an aside to Chomley, he added, "Perhaps you should order another bottle."

The man assessed the situation ruefully and quickly made his decision: his smile beamed and he grabbed a chair from another table and sat down almost in a single movement. "Delighted to," he said. He put out his hand to Chomley and said, "I'm John Hestlethwaite, one of Jimmy's old sparring partners."

Chomley was never good at judging these situations, but he found the intruder obnoxious for reasons that weren't entirely clear. With all the gravitas he could summon up, he pronounced, "Dick Chomley, scientist and author."

"Of course, *Egotism is Nature*."

"Yes," said Chomley proudly, even preeningly, the memory of

the ovation he had recently received reviving in his brain, "did you read it?"

"Oh yes, hugely entertaining, although I can't share all your opinions."

"Well, of course, arts and humanities are a little resistant."

"Arts and humanities?" said Hexham. "The man's a nuclear physicist. They say he'll be a Nobel Prize winner. But he's also a ghastly pinko-liberal, isn't that right, Johnny?" And he clapped the man on the back for good measure.

Chomley blushed.

"So what have you boys been talking about?" Johnny said, a little condescendingly, while tapping his wedding ring against his glass of wine.

"This and that. Pushkin," said Chomley.

"Pushkin?" said Johnny, sitting up with genuine surprise. "What interested you in him?"

"He was part negro," said Hexham.

"And Lord Hexham's son is going to do his Ph.D. on Pushkin, and Lord Hexham would prefer him to do something that would lead to a good job," Chomley clarified.

"Oh, I get it," said Johnny, "Lord Hexham has been coming out with his racist theories. Come on, Jimmy, do you never give up? So what's your latest: the blacks are responsible for your son's academic choices? Must be a plot. So, yeah, Pushkin was one-quarter black and he founded a literature. I would have thought that would be something you'd want to keep quiet about, Jimmy, given your views on the matter. Well consider this: his African grandfather was a mathematical genius and Peter the Great's adopted son. And there weren't that many Africans living in Russia at the time."

"Statistically insignificant," Hexham replied, his face darkening.

"Well, we all know your idiotic views on miscegenation. I hate to tell you, Jimmy, but it works like this: if you're a European and you worry about your children's genetic health, then you should marry a Nigerian, and if you're an African, you should marry a Swede or anybody else who is genetically distant from you. More generally of course, you should marry, if marry you must, anyone you want – someone you love, someone from your own community, of the same religion, whatever makes you and that other person comfortable."

"You're not seriously suggesting people should still let their religion decide who they marry?" asked Chomley.

"I didn't use the word 'should'. I don't care a damn who people marry. It would be good for society if more marriages were happy, but no one can know what'll work and what won't. It's a lottery, like most things in life. But I don't see why a shared religion shouldn't count, if it matters to the people in question. Some couples marry because they both like ballroom dancing or holidays in Italy or films by Laurel and Hardy. There are all tastes. I'm an atheist, but I have no desire to proselytise my atheism."

Chomley went silent.

"You see what he's like, Chomley," said Hexham, "the swine drives me crazy with his pinko ideas. I think he just likes winding me up."

"Listen, guys, my guests are beginning to arrive; I've got to leave you, but it's been great to have this little chat." Johnny turned to Chomley and smiled his well-judged, attractive but inscrutable smile, "Fancy meeting the great Dick Chomley. A real pleasure, and good that you're doing so well. I wanted to go to your lecture of course, but I had prior teaching commitments I simply couldn't get out of." He shook Chomley's hand politely and Hexham's with a degree of warmth. "Goodbye, you old bastard," he said, "I'll see you soon, no doubt."

"You can count on it," Hexham replied, "and I might just give you that slap around the head. You've been looking for it for long enough."

You might think that the drivel Chomley and Hexham speak is harmless drivel, but it's not. When two influential people meet in a bar or restaurant to talk drivel, it is always important drivel. A Spanish philosopher once said that what intellectuals say in one generation will become common parlance in three or four generations' time. Nietzsche's glorification of war led a few decades later to a terrible slogan: "War: the only way to clean up the world" and a decade or two after that the world wars started. The racist theories being unearthed by Neo-Darwinism could lead us down the same route that Gobineau's did. The victims might be different, but the results the same. Perhaps for now we can fight them with patience, argument and good manners, as Johnny Hestlewhaite did, but these will not always work.

When their eyes met after Johnny's departure, both Chomley and Hexham felt a degree of embarrassment. It would have been interesting to see how their conversation would have developed from there, but quite suddenly they were aware that someone had sat down on Johnny's chair. Chomley looked at the young man in his late teens and recognised his features. He then looked at Hexham and even he could read the conflicting emotions in his lordship's expression: anger, pride and perhaps even love.

"Chomley, let me introduce the son I was telling you about: he's called Trevor. A chip off the old block, don't you think?"

"Yes," Chomley muttered.

"What can I do for you, Trevor?"

"I've been looking for you all over the place. They said you were at the lecture, so I went down there and saw your Mercedes – so I waited in the car park – then this gentleman came up just exactly when I was about to approach you – I followed you to the restaurant, but didn't have the guts to go in – I went back to the car park and there was lots of people running round looking for your Professor Chomley – so I went back to the restaurant – this time I went in and blow me, this other geezer comes up and sits down – they let me stay and I waited for him to finish – well, here I am."

"They're probably after your blood, Chomley," said Hexham, without a trace of regret. However, there may well have been a suggestion that he would like to be left alone with his son. If there was, Chomley did not detect it.

All three sat in silence. Chomley was curious, the young man clearly had something difficult to say and Hexham appeared to be in shock, but he was the first to speak: "This is a pleasant surprise, but I sense there is a reason. You're not in trouble, are you?"

Trevor visibly relaxed: "Not at all. Quite the opposite. Basically, I'm in love."

Lord Hexham would never have made such an announcement to his father, when he was in his teens, and here was this son he barely knew telling him about his intimate emotions. He was both repelled and attracted by this news.

Trevor was now smiling innocence: "I have a picture of her." He opened his wallet and took out a small photograph, which he handed to his father.

Lord Hexham stared at it in stunned silence for at least a minute: "She's very pretty," he said, passing the photo to his fellow diner, "don't you think, Chomley?"

Chomley too seemed a little surprised or possibly bemused.

"Where's she from?" asked Hexham.

"Chad."

"Chad? Very interesting. Pushkin's grandfather is thought to have come from Chad."

Trevor pushed his confusion away and pursued the purpose of his visit. "We've a lot to celebrate. She has just got her Indefinite Leave to Remain."

Chomley was still examining the picture of a smiling young woman in European dress standing in front of a large building, probably an educational establishment. Forgetting the sound advice to keep quiet in all family situations, he allowed himself to say, "Another asylum seeker, then."

"And you have a problem with that?" Hexham boomed.

"What the hell!" said Chomley, "you're hardly the one to ..."

"I don't know what you're going to say, Chomley, but you'd better not say it. And if you'll excuse me, I have a few things I want to say to my son."

He turned to his son and said, "This is fantastic news, Trevor. And it's great that you felt you could tell me. You want some help – probably financial. I hope that's what it is, because I can tell you now that it's not a problem – not at all. Does she have legal costs?"

"No, she got assistance on that, and we dealt with the rest. No, it's nothing as serious as that. It's just that I'd like to take her on holiday. I'd like to take her to Italy. I've always wanted to go, and she has had such a tough life. And for the last two years we couldn't go outside London together."

"Is that all?" said the beaming Lord Hexham, "then I'll write the cheque immediately." Clearly delighting in his own generosity, he took out his chequebook and his fountain pen. His handwriting was laborious, contributing to the suspense that led up to the final flourish of his signature. He tore it off and handed it to his son, who stared at it in disbelief.

"My God, that's too much, Dad. We could stay in five-star hotels for a month with that."

"Then stay in five-star hotels," his father laughed. "All you have to do is come and see us at our home when you get back. Bring your girlfriend. We'll be delighted to see her. Don't worry about my wife. She has known about your existence for years, and got over it long ago. She's a good woman and she'll welcome you with open arms. As will your brother. This is wonderful news."

"I don't know what to say," said Trevor.

"Then don't. Just get out of here. Have fun. And make sure you come and see us. You know that's what I've always wanted. We want to see you both, remember. Go where you want, and have an adventure. And get the hell out of here, and don't keep the lady waiting."

The boy left. The father watched him go all the way to the restaurant door, and then turned back towards Chomley. "Well, that's a turn-up for the books," he smiled.

Chomley was glum and feeling excluded. More seriously he hadn't understood the nature of the encounter he had just witnessed. "Lord Hexham, I can't say there's a lot of intellectual coherence in the way you live your life."

"Listen Chomley, that's all very well but you can take your intellectual coherence and stick it up your arse. Has anybody told you you're a monomaniac and a bore? I don't care about what I used to say. I like this girl and I like her for a very selfish reason: she has brought me together with my son. He never asked me for anything before; that was always his mother's fault. I had to go and see him – beg him – and he was sullen and distrustful. And now he's come to see me of his own free will and he'll come again if I play my cards right. I was wrong, Chomley; is that what you want to hear? What's Chad to my sons? It's just down the road. My father would have been angry if I'd married a Scot or an Irishwoman – definitely an Irishwoman. The world has changed and I'm just a silly old fool. I'm just a molecular biologist, a very good one but not God Almighty. What do I know? You think I'm a racist, because I said all those things about the intelligence of negroes. Well, you're right: that is racism, but at least I said what I thought – more because of the weight of my upbringing than any intellectual thing."

"Am I interested in your family life?" Chomley asked with unfamiliar steel and his sarcasm underscored.

"No, this isn't about my family life any more; it's about intellectual method. In those drab little books of yours with their quite unscientific methodology – if you don't mind me saying – you fail to understand that in those areas of human thought we can only hope to organise our ignorance and give it a little shape. That's a huge task, and the results have to be modest. What I do and Johnny does is science and the results are very concrete. In other areas of my life, theory is one thing and experience another, and experience has the upper hand. When he showed me the picture of that girl, I knew that I wanted to help her too. Maybe the relationship won't last; young love rarely does, but I won't be the one to drive her away and she'll be the means by which I get my son into my life."

He stood up, gathered his things together, and smiled at Chomley: "I can be an arse, I know. You've had a rotten time. There's more to life than a good lunch, and a good lunch is not primarily the food on the table; it is the sum of the relationships that surround it. Do you want me to pay the bill?"

"No need for that."

Hexham practically danced out of the restaurant.

Chomley paid at the desk near the door, lifted his coat from the rack and slipped it on as he stepped out onto the street. There was a fine drizzle which, given his mood, depressed him. Hexham, presumably, had found it refreshing.

Bearing Up Life's Burdens Merrily

I woke one morning with an unusual zest for life. "We must go into town today," I told my wife as I threw the tea bags in the bin – or rather, attempted to, because they missed and, on falling to the floor, stained the side of the target. "I feel that it could be something of an event, a memorable day in our life together. Too long have we let the grass grow under our feet; too long have we coasted through the months and years happily eating fried food and watching the TV; too long have we forgotten that life is an adventure and we're here to feel and to test the exceptionality of our existence."

"I agree," she said and she usually did, "a trek is what we need, to give a special feeling to this day."

"I'm glad you agree," I said – although I took her acquiescence for granted, I did not like to give the appearance of doing so.

"However," she added after some thought, "I don't think we should be rash. Are you not of the opinion that it would be sensible to take the sofa as well?"

"I do," I said, quite surprised by my wife's unexpected sagacity, "I think it would be a most judicious precaution."

Quite exhausted by our intellectual labours, we decided not to take the next bus, but wait for the 11.30. I made more tea and again failed to get the tea bags into the bin, even though I customised it long ago by ripping off the lid.

"Darling," I said – ever my uxorious self, "the bin is in the wrong position. You're making me throw the tea bags on the floor. Tomorrow morning, could you please remember to shift the bin six inches to the right, and there'll be no more problems with the tea bags."

"Of course, my love," she answered absently, while spinning the tassel on a large ballpoint pen with pictures of apparently generic castles and cathedrals, which someone had brought back from Krakow.

I handed her a cup of warm, milky tea and sat down heavily on the sofa. I smiled happily at my wife and enjoyed the splendid familiarity of our sofa's soft cushioning effect. Nowhere else on earth could I have found such comfort as this, which was provided above all by the presence of my wife and my sofa.

After an hour in the pleasant company of them both, it was decided that the time had come to set off on our adventure. We did discuss the possibility of another short postponement, but pertinacity won out and we set off with our sofa.

When the bus came, we immediately encountered difficulty in getting the sofa on the bus. In this we were particularly hindered by the presence of a stainless-steel bar running vertically between the floor and the ceiling of the bus, presumably for people not good on their pins to grab hold of as they embark on and alight from the bus. I noticed that the bar was secured by three screws at each end, so I took out my screwdriver to remove the unnecessary obstacle.

The bus driver started to protest, and I felt that he was taking a lot on himself. Actually what he said was quite shocking: "Ye're no bringin' that mingin' auld trash aun ma bus."

This demonstrated the lack of common courtesy in our corrupt modern society. My father, whose blessed career I chose to follow in almost every respect, was also in the habit of taking a sofa on the bus, and the response was always much more measured, along such lines as "Excuse me sur, there's a corporation directive that specifically forbids the conveyance of all items of furniture on corporation buses." That's progress for you.

I returned my screwdriver to my inside pocket with the air of a man who had been prevented from doing his duty. "Clearly people around here have some very strange priorities," I exclaimed with the joy of the outraged, "if this were a free country, then its citizens would be allowed to take their sofas wherever they want: museums, ancient castles, cathedrals, universities, football pitches – almost anywhere one would like to enjoy the pleasures of a comfortable seat and the occasional snooze. But it appears that in this country you cannot even take them on the bus."

For some reason the passengers already on the bus found all of this highly amusing, but I spoke in earnest – spoke from the heart.

My wife, who is always my support, put her arm in mine and led me away from further altercation. We removed two legs of the sofa from the first step on the bus, and as soon as we'd done so, the ill-mannered driver threw the gear stick into first and rushed the bus away, even before the door stopped closing. We felt ourselves enveloped in a rush of damp, diesel-laden air that brought with it the cold admonition of the conventional.

"There's nothing for it," I declared in part to my wife and in part to any bystanders wishing to hear my forthright speech, which potentially could rank alongside the Gettysburg Address or the Declaration of Arbroath, "we shall have to strive alone and neglected, we shall have to carry this burden in the name of liberty itself, we shall have to fight for the ancient Caledonian right to sleep in comfort wherever we should wish. There is no law of trespass in Scotland or on its buses."

Greatness is not given to every ingenious soul; greatness requires luck and, as luck would have it, my only audience was an irascible ram who, missing his daily dose of rain, was bothered by the pleasant April sun. He studied me with disdain and then furious at my intolerable presence, started to butt a wooden gate repeatedly in some vain attempt to break it and perhaps pursue me.

With every blow, the metal hinges and bolt rattled loudly like a warning and my wife said, "I think perhaps we should get on with it." She then lifted one end of the sofa to show her impatience.

It's a good three hundred yards from the bus stop to the centre of the town – well, I have perhaps exaggerated, more of a large village with a post office where you can buy milk and a newspaper.

Such a feat of endurance should not be undertaken lightly, but understanding my wife's apprehension, I decided not to linger and lifted my end too.

I feel that before narrating further aspects of our adventure, I should inform the reader of what kind of woman was my consort and companion, for without her I would not have achieved all the great things I have achieved in life.

Like me, she was in her mid forties and like me, she stood about five and a half foot in her stocking feet. But while I tended towards a slightly heavier frame, she was sylph-like, although some might have uncharitably said that she tended towards haggardness. Her hair was long, curly and prematurely white, some might have said dishevelled. Whatever some might have said, she was for me the woman most perfect in this world, and I considered myself the luckiest man in the world for as long as she continued to do what I asked of her and did it with a good grace.

I think you'll be surprised and somewhat impressed to hear that she was an admiral's daughter. It's true that an admiral is not quite as grand as it may sound. He was probably one of those sedentary admirals who stuck to his desk and never went to sea. One thing was clear: he was no judge of character. For reasons that are still unclear, he took against me and threatened to disown his daughter if she married me. Worse, he actually kept his word, in spite of the fact that she was his only child. When he died, he left all his fortune to St. Boswald's Hospice for Injured Naval Officers, a charity so rich financially and so bereft of potential beneficiaries that it hands out sinecures to young men of good family. In other words, it doesn't so much help naval officers fallen on hard times as unemployed and feckless public schoolboys. In spite of his nefarious behaviour and inability to perceive a true case of hardship when it appeared before him, we kept a photo of the rogue in our home, as my wife remained and presumably remains inordinately fond of him, and I liked to indulge her from time to time.

In the picture, he wore a hat a bit like a ship turned upside down. I pointed out to my wife that he wasn't wearing it in the proper position, but she explained to me that in Her Majesty's

Royal Navy they wear these hats "fore and aft" and not "across the beam" as do pirates and Napoleon. Clearly foreigners and ruffians cannot know the correct position for headwear. I was quite impressed by my wife's knowledge of such terminology, but I doubt she knew the difference between a destroyer and a battleship. Women have difficulty with such concepts, but in those days I liked to spend an afternoon in the company of *Jane's Fighting Ships*. I was probably more expert than her father, when it came to such fundamental matters, but I was willing to bend to their greater knowledge of sartorial questions.

After a hundred yards of lugging a sofa, I was in a bit of a sweat. In my youth, I was considered an Adonis and my performance on the running track was well known to many, even in distant places like Glasgow and Edinburgh. But years of hard work and setbacks of all kinds had taken their toll. I was not the man I had once been, but inside the youthful flame of resolve and audacity still burnt.

Still a hundred yards is a hundred yards, and so I intimated to my wife to lower her end of the sofa by dropping my end abruptly on the pavement. She sat on the armrest at her end, took out a packet of cigarettes and proceeded to smoke in her nervous manner, one puff quickly followed by another, as though she were blowing a balloon the wrong way rather than partaking of a pleasure. In the meantime I lay my head just below her and swung my legs onto the other armrest. Almost immediately my mind sank into a deep and luxurious sleep, such as only the virtuous can enjoy.

When he was young, he painted and did so with a passion. When he woke in the morning his mind would start to buzz. He was not a great artist and possibly could never have become one. But neither was he devoid of talent, or at least that is what I am told by those who understand these things (as a narrator, I am as confused as you are: don't read my jottings, if you want to know the absolute truth about anything, or how to live your life usefully and successfully; there are libraries full of that stuff, while all I want to do is deepen your sense of being lost in a maze you never wanted to enter, because you and I, reader, detest such puzzles and parlour games, particularly those in which there has to be a winner and loser, with the exception of chess, because there always has to be an exception; we like to deceive ourselves that life isn't like these stupid games – that it is something nobler).

So he was not successful, possibly because he insisted on painting with paint on a surface and producing images both figurative and abstract. If, on the other hand, he had dried tadpoles in the oven, dissected them and reconstituted them haphazardly in the shape of diaphanous butterflies, he would have been visited by a rich man who would have said, "I am a rich man, and I will make you rich and myself richer. We'll found a new artistic movement and we'll call it Mart-Art, which, if you haven't already guessed it, is the art of the market – a sensitive being who thinks much more cleverly than all of us put together. A godlike creature, one might say."

But this conversation did not take place, because he had this fixation with how paint glues itself to a surface and fools us into seeing things we can't understand and understanding things we hitherto have failed to see.

While I slept and floated through the sluggish dreamlessness of a post-meridiem nap, my wife must have left me to do some shopping. I awoke and saw an elegant gentleman in a suit. He was photographing me, and my immediate reaction was one of indignation, but then I heard his words: "Excellent artwork, reclining artist on a couch. A statement, I would say, on domesticity in the early twenty-first century. Here in the middle of nowhere: this guy's a genius."

I was heartened by what he said, but also a little confused. "Who are you?" I asked.

"Here's my card," he laughed superciliously, "I'm an art dealer. Highly successful one, I should tell you."

"Mart-Art?"

"Good God, no," he scoffed in a manner that immediately revealed an upper-crusty background. Posh school and all that. Probably knew the prime minister. "Living concept art – that's my thing. I believe that art should be fashioned not just from organic material, but from live organic material – preferably humanoid. In your case, the 'oid' is entirely necessary."

"Conceptual art? You mean like cows cut in two and formaldehyde?"

"No, no, bisected beasts are old hat, I'm afraid. I'm at the cutting edge."

I confess that, although an educated man, I could not entirely follow his drift – or indeed a word he said. His irritating manner was countervailed by a forceful notion that there might be a few quid in this encounter for me. I sat up and stared the man in the eye, to show him that I was not a man to be trifled with and that I was quite assured of my right to set down my sofa anywhere on the pedestrian highway and use it as I wished. "Are you, by any chance, interested in buying this artwork? The idea only came to me this morning."

"I am, dear friend. I am very interested."

"How much?"

"A thousand smackeroos per diem!" he smiled grandly, obviously enjoying his affected turn of phrase.

"Per diem?"

"Per day, if you like."

"I know that. I am an educated man," I said, "but what do you mean? Are you renting the sofa for a thousand pounds a day?"

"No, that would be ridiculous," he laughed again, quite taken aback. "The sofa, if you don't mind me saying so, is almost worthless. You are, as I'm sure you know better than I do, an integral part of the artwork. Without your good self, the concept cannot work. I therefore need you to be at my gallery in High Wycombe from nine in the morning until six o'clock in the evening. And I need you dressed pretty much as you are now. Very clever, how you did that."

"Did what?"

"Choose that clothing. Very ironic in a fashionably post-modern kind of way. They'll come up from London to see you."

"But …"

"You'll be famous."

"Can I sleep on the sofa occasionally?"

The gentleman gave my question a great deal of thought before suddenly making his decision: "Yes, that could work. I like it."

"And will I be able to watch television?"

"I'm afraid not," he replied without hesitation.

You see how we're the playthings of fate? This poor man was being offered the chance to do the kind of thing he refused to do two decades earlier at great cost to himself and his partner, and the new terms offered by this man were decidedly worse and very humiliating. But the money was good and sooner or later everyone must make a compromise with society as it actually is. Those who don't bend to their times deserve everything that happens to them.

That was the moment when my wife returned. I have to say that she was brighter than I have ever given her credit for. She immediately sensed that something was not quite kosher, if you know what I mean. Here was this smartly dressed man who had now extracted a wad of money from his pocket, and he was telling me what to do, as though he were born to command and I to be commanded.

"Who is this creep?" she asked.

"An art dealer."

"What does he want?"

"To buy my artwork."

Here she brightened. "You mean he has seen your paintings. Why didn't you tell me?"

"No, he's going to buy this work." I pointed to the sofa. "This item of organically living art."

"Live concept art," the gentleman corrected me with a sneer.

"And I'm an integral part of the exhibit. So I've got to go down to England – to a place called High Wycombe near London where they'll come and see me. And I'll be rich. And you too, of course."

"So you've sold him our sofa, if I'm not mistaken."

"No. I've hired out my exhibit, which consists of myself and the sofa, but I have the more important role."

"It gets worse and worse. Can't you see he's jerking you around?"

"Do you know this woman?" asked the gentleman, who was now becoming impatient.

"Well," I replied, "I can't say that I do. She looks a lot like the woman I've been married to for the last twenty-five years, but she doesn't behave like her at all."

"Listen, you dickhead," my wife pronounced with uncommon rudeness, "I married you because I believe in you and your work. We made sacrifices, and I respected you for sticking to your principles. I put up with you, when you became depressed and could never get your arse up off this bloody sofa of yours. And now when we've grown old together, you're going to throw it all up to go off with this ponce to High Fuckem."

"Don't take it so personally, dear," I protested calmly, even though my blood was boiling and I couldn't believe the change from her usual demeanour.

"You haven't touched a paintbrush in fifteen years. You gave up on life and I stood by you. And now this! I'm going home for a cup of tea, and you can do what the fuck you want." And that was the last time I saw her.

The art dealer was called Charles Devon, and sadly our artist had never heard my grandmother's favourite expression: "Never trust a man named after a county". He was true to his word and did pay a thousand pounds a day for the installation, but the artist had to pay most of it back for the rental of the dealer's penthouse in High Wycombe and the costs that came with the new persona that was imposed on the poor man. After the long day lying on the sofa, the artist generally had to go home, shower and dress in black tie. He was then expected to quaff red wine at various cultural events, where he recycled all the drivel he'd learnt from Mr. Devon and was rewarded with glances of approval and wonderment.

Life's defeats and life's successes, how they both weigh you down! I ask myself whether I would have done better to compromise or

– let's use the word I've been avoiding – sell out, back when I was young, to those who can afford to buy you. Or whether I should have followed my wife's advice and kept aloof from this world and its shabby trade-offs. We could have continued in our state of glorious suspended animation.

I now enjoy greater recognition than I have ever enjoyed in my life – in fact it is the only recognition of any kind that I have ever received. And what for? What exactly do I do to earn these looks of high regard not from the hoi polloi, but the cognoscenti of the art world? I recline, lie, sleep and occasionally snore on a battered blue sofa in clothes that I have now come to detest, but which once belonged to me as much as my own skin. They think that I wear them as an affectation, as a statement on the human condition, but the affectation is, I think, the black tie I wear in the evening. I have almost become part of those who judge and comment upon the lives of others, who smile weakly with worldly wisdom and carry lightly the grandness of their designs.

The lack of authenticity in everything I do started to feel bearable, as I soon realised after the initial shock that this job, if I can call it that, is leading somewhere. Eventually I will be accepted as an artist of a kind, and this will emancipate me from my servitude to young Devon. Why do they smile at my reclining self? Where is the supposed subtle irony? It is in my wide girth and the vacant stare of a defeated man. But by making an artefact of my former self, I am freeing myself from it. I now eat low-fat yoghurt and go jogging at weekends; my stomach recedes and my confidence grows. I tell anecdotes and smoothly syllabise the words I speak, giving the impression of great thoughtfulness. People laugh at my jokes, although I suspect they seldom understand them. And they fill my glass with intoxicating conviviality. I will succeed.

But succeed in what? The question still returns – and every time it burdens me with increasing cynicism and worldliness and, more recently, inflicts a tiny fear which also grows so slowly, but grows nonetheless. That fear is the fear of losing all this, although I'm not sure what "this" is, or whether it has any intrinsic worth.

A young artist came to see me the other day and he brought

a work of exquisite clarity: a portrait of a young woman playing chess outside a café. It was set in a Mediterranean country and she had a warm liveliness even as her concentration on the game isolated her from a colourful, motley company of onlookers. The painting sent a shiver down my back, and I could have cried: that was what I wanted to do, if only I had the skill to do it. I had once come close enough to the skill required, for me to appreciate it fully. But I gave nothing away, and the young man was so in awe of me that I could feel his craving for recognition like a magnetic force I needed to resist. But why did he crave? Because I am suddenly prominent in artistic circles? Doesn't he see through the sham and shambles of this art trade? The idiot got everything he deserved. "Is that a woman's face or an item of footwear?" I asked. "Her eyes are dead and her thin mouth like the lace of a shoe. If you must paint, I suggest you restrict yourself to still lifes." And I felt no guilt at all, but I did feel a sickly pleasure in crushing another human being's desire to succeed where I had failed. In the evening as I went to bed slightly drunk, I thought to myself that when I was depressed and isolated and living with my wife, I would never have been capable of such an act of wilful cruelty whose only purpose was the exercise of cruelty itself.

There is, I suppose, always success in failure and failure in success. But my success is based on something inauthentic to me, which brings an extra burden of failure. How many times I dreamt of a dealer discovering my paintings, and then this fool appears and turns my depressed self into a living artwork.

I detest Devon for having commandeered my life and having made it better – in a way. Despair removes all concern about the future and throws its victim into the arms of the present, which has some comforts, but hope creates the oppressiveness of infinite possibilities – of too many plausible futures. I think the main reason I stay with Devon is to find out how far this absurdity can go, and that creates the intoxication of even greater absurdities. I'm not an artist; I am an *objet d'art*. If what I do is art, then Devon is the artist and he made me, but for his own reasons he maintains the fiction that I am the creative one.

He could never understand why I would not like to live a lie, because he lives a lie and lives it happily and with great gusto. He calls me "dear friend", as though he were the older man. He buys my clothes and deducts the bills from my pay. He invites leading journalists to interview me, filling them with extraordinary stories of my prowess, and then calls me a "chump" when he comes round to complain about something late in the evening. Everything he does repels me, and everything he does binds me to him. His is a very sophisticated form of economic exploitation, and mine is a very peculiar form of alienation.

And once the years will have folded away, *The Guardian* will write the following obituary:

The Guardian | Friday 28 April 2045

Robert Scott

The reclining genius who invented Live Concept Art and became the byword for refine-ment and sophistication in the 2010s

Robert Scott, who has died after an extended illness at the age of 85, rose to prominence in 2013 and is generally credited with found-ing the Live Concept Movement which dramatically broke into the British art scene in that crucial year. Known as "Rabby" by his friends in London, he was a col-ourful character well liked by most of his peers, in spite of his fondness for the bottle and occasional spats with his fellow artists.

Born in Bridge of Allan in 1960, Scott appears to have broken off all relations with his family after his move south to High Wycombe in 2013. He never spoke to his wife after he left her and went in search of Charles Devon to pitch his ideas for revolutionising British art once the Mart-Art movement had gone into the doldrums. Devon, then a young, ambitious but relatively unknown art dealer in the prov-inces, was quick to understand the brilliance of Scott's new ideas. The story is that he had Scott eat huge quantities of junk food for months before he would allow his protégé to launch his first and most celebrated artwork, "Couch Potato", in which the artist himself reclined on a ludicrously tattered old sofa. Some considered the sofa and the cheap and gaudy clothing he wore for the installation to be somewhat overstated, but they failed to understand Scott's subtle humour, which says so much about the human condition without resorting to extravagant complexities. Not without reason he has been referred to as the Raymond Carver of the art world.

Devon claimed that Scott spent weeks trying to persuade him of his ideas, but Devon found it difficult to picture the lithe and dapper Scott playing the part of an ignorant and slothful unemployed person who does little other than watch daytime TV. But the public who first saw Scott reclining on that now infamous sofa must have thought he was born for the part. That was the power of Scott's chameleon nature.

At the age of sixty, Scott married Jean Turvy, the model who was thirty-five years his junior. She too was a trailblazer and the first of the "petite poseurs" who ushered in a new taste in female beauty. Theirs was a short and troubled relationship, although they did have two children who were mainly brought up by Turvy's mother.

Scott was often a controversial figure and he fell out badly with Devon ten years after they met. The cause of this rift is still unknown, as they both refused to talk about it. Scott managed to avoid all mention of Devon in his autobiography, or of his first wife Augusta, the daughter of Admiral Pennington who commanded the task force against insurgents in Dhofar in the early seventies. Augusta, very much a child of the sixties, wrote a satirical novel on the Mart-Art milieu which was largely ignored when she published it in 2018 but has since achieved cult status in some artistic circles. She died twelve years ago in Paignton.

Scott was awarded the OBE in 2033 for services to art and culture. He is survived by his second wife and his children, Dominic and Sarah.

James Hautiduns

Robert MacLeod Ferguson Scott, artist, born Saturday 9 January 1960; died Thursday 27 April 2045.

Lives Both Sundered and Adjoined

This is not the story of stars, ocean deeps, magma flows and inner cores – just the story of our intangible passions that multiply like galaxies, but with more erratic energy. The constellations of our loves and hates, of our ambitions, gratitudes, kindnesses, obscure sexual needs, quieted desires, lost hopes, aesthetic obsessions, and so much more that sparks from our brains and appears to leave no trace. Appears, I say, for all that humanity has done was done through those sparks – the atoms of emotions that fly through the universe of human habitation but cannot reach beyond it, any more than sound can travel in a vacuum.

You think me foolish to take on this task? Who can disentangle this maelstrom of random forces and petulant emotion? Who can judge chaos that has no purpose, no guiding principle and no pattern of justice? Why don't I describe an exotic murder in great detail and lead you through the rational process that uncovers the perpetrator? All would be unravelled and reassuring. Why don't I tell you of strange people only motivated by power, sex and money? Real people are so much more unreasonable, and we can have little time for them. Surely I could hold you with a simple story of revenge in which horrible acts justify so many others? Forgiveness is out of season.

Sadly I'm not interested in those silly fantasies whose allure is proof again of our erratic souls. What fascinates me is the real, which defies all understanding and to which I can only add a few more perplexities of my own.

If it's all so unknowable, I can only explain a little of its wonders by isolating tiny examples – and in choosing my examples, is it not right that I should rest my attention on one of our finer emotions? In an age in which the scabrous is mistaken for profundity, allow me to talk of love which, restricted as it is to the parts of the earth's crust not covered by water and snow but not necessarily devoid of them either, is greater in its emotional expanse than several universes. I hear you clicking your tongue in disapproval at my sentimentality – I too am conscious of this hideous faux pas – but listen to my story first and then tell me that I exaggerate. You will not, because we know what it is, even when – slave to cynicism – we spend a lifetime denying its existence.

There's the youth who yearns to save his youthfulness – to hoard it like a passion and cash it in for a splendid old age, when he will continue to hoard, because hoarding will have become his inescapable essence. His pots and potions, his diets and work-outs, disguise the fact that he is fading, like us all. While he looks in the mirror and gloats at the ripple of his abdominal muscles and his pecs, he doesn't notice that he's drowning in the icy pool of self-love. He is a victim of his time, which thinks it has defeated time. He doesn't see the parabola of existence, short and curved like the broken back of senescence and decrepitude. He founds his life on land below sea level and spends it furiously building dams to keep out the greater fury of the restless, deathly sea.

There's the old lady who lives alone with her cats and reads every nineteenth-century novel she can lay her hands on: Dickens of course, always Dickens with his multitude of voices, Thackeray, Eliot, Trollope and the Russians. She lives in another century, which lives again in her mind: she suffers, weeps, laughs, longs and learns from all those many people imagined long ago in accents different and stilted now, and she lives perhaps a fuller life than some in this small sample and beyond.

There's the middle-aged manager at the bank who travels from branch to branch, troubleshooting and sorting local disputes with Solomonic zeal. Always and even while he dispenses judgements and coolly resolves disputes others take to heart, he keeps his eyes busy on another task: appraising the shapeliness of female forms squeezed into tight and tartaned suits, and choosing which should share his bed for a few nights of fun that become a way of life. Fun is drudgery when sequentially repeated on and on till the spring of original desire is quite dry but still imperiously demands that its needs be met. Lothario forgets but somewhere still recalls a purpose which is not only this. His love of women can no longer be love of a woman. Or does he delude himself in every case that this is the one? Three nights in his imagined world belong to lives of imagined closeness wedded to an ideal ardour each more ideal than all the others that have failed. Can humans indulge in such self-deceit? Of course, it is the larger part of what we do.

There's the accountant who most carefully keeps the books of his own assets and liabilities, who checks his statements as they come and checks again to feel the fullness of his moneyed self. He lives in times most suited to himself, and is the archetype of our modern philosophy – a man who closely adheres to his economic self-interest carefully assessed with skill and knowledge of what he speaks. He loves those figures on the page that bulge and lengthen like a promise of future health, like paradise postponed, but here on earth.

There's the mother who waiting at the school gate gently rocks the pushchair with later offspring loaded and ready to wail. She loves with a love so great it heartens us and give us hope for future years in these most hopeless times. She renews, and in renewing fades so fast her sisters scoff and call her dumb. Her patience is the fragile plant on which our societies all are built, and its dying embers produce so many outcomes we cannot list them all: pride, envy, desolation, regret and anger at unexpected ingratitude that cannot fail to come.

There's the driver who delivers cockles for the master of a gang – of poor souls. People who trudge on beaches bared by the tide and pick the slimy black fruit of sand and sea. They sleep cramped and huddled in a foul and frigid flat steeped in the fatigue of fragmented human lives. The driver is paid by the delivery and always speeds to fund his family in Morocco – one like so many others whose poverty carries all the weight of progress. When you live your life as fast as the driver, you do not live at all. Where is the pause to nourish an existence condemned by circumstance to brevity?

There's the couple: he a thirty-year-old English teacher and she, two years older, a translator of legal documents when her cystic fibrosis allows her to work. The disease's moods govern their daily lives, and yet the eleven years they have lived together have been much happier than most relationships are. A consistent happiness, but the disease's slow, erratic but inexorable development threatens it.

He wanted to say that they were alone against the world, against others, against society and above all against cruel nature. But instead he said pathetically, "I couldn't live without you."

"I know, but you will have to learn," she responded with a mixture of irritation and compassion. She felt his pain – his tongue-tied pain – and it provoked in her a desire for merciless frankness. "You will have another lover – more than one, I expect."

"How can you?"

"Easy. A dose of reality is required. There is a reason why they look askance at us. Because they, like you, think that ideal love is a constant, but no such love exists. Love lives in a moment, and if it is rekindled, it can survive into the following moment and eventually into weeks, months and years. I don't doubt your love – I never doubt it for a second. I can feel it and am strengthened by its intensity, but no amount of rekindling will keep a fire alight if there's not oxygen left in the air. When I am gone, your love will have no oxygen. For a while you will feel as if you're suffocating. You'll hate people for coming round to commiserate and you'll hate them when they don't. Very slowly you'll start to breathe more freely. The periods in which you'll forget me will lengthen."

Here he objected angrily, but she would not have it.

"Let me finish! There's nothing wrong in all this. It's entirely natural. Sooner or later you'll have to pull out a photograph to remember what I look like. Some years later still, you won't seek me out, but when you happen across a photo in a drawer or between the pages of a book, I'll stare out at you from a past that'll feel like another life. Remarried with children and their daily problems, you'll wonder what all the fuss was about. You'll marvel at the passion and think yourself a fool."

Tears ran down his face. Their cause was not self-pity, compassion or sorrow; it was fierce, blood-boiling anger that could find no other outlet. The world we inhabit is so hard, unjust and unremitting. In fiction and in childhood, some *Deus ex machina* or parent is meant to step in eventually and say, "You've had your punishment, order has been re-established and now you can go out and play happily ever after." But this would never happen. She wanted to savour the time she had left, and wanted him to forget for now the long years of life that would follow her death. She was not jealous of the women to come; she wanted him to live in the present as she was obliged to do.

"It's unfair. Unfair on you," he protested weakly.

"Life isn't fair," she laughed, "didn't your parents teach you that? The most important lesson they can give. But life mitigates its gross unfairness by distributing hidden, paradoxical compensations. We have no need to burden ourselves with property, as do so many of our age. No mortgage, no collections of expensive porcelain, no investment plans. We live for the moment, knowing that there will not be that many. Perhaps I'm being selfish: pensions are of no concern to me, but they will be for you. We should live for the maximum pleasure any moment can give. Right now, I'm feeling good. I think I'm fit enough to walk five hundred yards and pretend that I could go further. We do what gives us pleasure. No sucking up to get promotion, no pleasing parents just to satisfy their ambitions for us, no kidding on that I can defeat this disease."

"You can. Medical science ..."

"Don't go there. If things turn out better than expected, fine, but I'm not living my life in the belief that one day I'll be pruning the roses in my garden at the age of eighty-five. I want to get the most out of the life I know I'll have. Not big things but small and many of them. Just now, I'd like to go to that piano bar on the avenue."

"Let's go then." They laughed as they put their coats on. He feigned misery and said, "Your negativity is a real killer."

She took his head between her hands in a manner that belied the weakness in her arms, and he allowed her to draw his head towards her so that she could place a brief but extravagantly passionate kiss on his thin lips. "You're a prick," she said, "but you're my prick."

"It's good to be wanted," he laughed again, and they walked out onto the street, whose dampness glistened now an expanse of unvarying blue had pushed away the mottled monochrome clouds. Hope, like the Glasgow weather, is an unstable condition. She hugged his arm and gave him a look that unnecessarily reassured him that she had only been joking. "I'm the one who couldn't go on without you. I was falling and you caught me. You've made life sweet." He smiled his embarrassment by way of a reply.

An elderly woman stepped out of a garden and addressed them in a commanding Kelvinside accent, the dreary vowels stretched as though it were an effort to force them out. "Have you seen a cat? A white one. It has a torn ear – from fights, you know. It's called Herodotus." The final item of information was entirely redundant, unless the cat could speak. More likely the woman simply wanted it to be made known that her cat was special and therefore deserving of an exalted name. They looked at her in surprise and immediately assessed her as dotty but amiable.

"We haven't seen any cats, I'm afraid," he asserted so firmly, you'd have thought that he'd left the house with the express purpose of checking and monitoring all feline presences along that stretch of road. "We'll keep an eye out for him. Rest assured," he added condescendingly.

"Oh, don't worry too much," she said. "I'm not. At least not yet. The little rogue usually comes back home when he's hungry."

They started to walk, but she stopped them immediately. "Have you read Thackeray?" she asked.

They said that they hadn't.

"You should, you know. He's very good."

He asked the old lady if this author writes detective stories, and she laughed. His girlfriend said she would look him up when she was next in Waterstone's, but the old lady's mind had moved on.

"You look such a nice young couple. In love, I hope. You probably think I'm a silly old woman stopping you on the street and talking to you like this. No one talks any more, you know. I was born before the days of television and computers, you see. When I was a child, people talked to each other incessantly. About absolutely nothing. It was wonderful. Don't you think? You probably don't."

They were, in fact, lost for words. The old lady could not have known that they were desperately searching for them, but they would not come.

"I understand," the old lady said. "I'm keeping you back. It has been lovely meeting you. You know where my house is now. Drop in for a cup of tea any time you want."

The old lady then turned purposefully, as though she too had a pressing engagement, and walked with great dignity back into her garden where a rubber kneeler and a trowel lay on the grass close to a partially weeded flower bed.

They exchanged a confidential smirk and continued their walk. A baby was screaming as though it had finally understood the heroism of mortals and saw before it the great hill of life it had to climb. More probably colic was working its monstrous magic.

The mother stopped and walked round to the front of the pushchair, where she unstrapped the baby and lifted it up tenderly. All the while, a boy of about nine was explaining to her the complicated plot of the latest Ben Ten movie. She nodded to him absently at intervals, devoting the rest of her time to the more complex task of cooing and bouncing the baby.

"I'd never want a sprog," she told her boyfriend. He looked less convinced. "You're mad," she added.

As they got close, the mother looked up and muttered an

apology, probably over the amount of pavement she was taking up. Her face was young, but her eyes were old. She was alone in so much company.

As they chatted about children and the darkness of the world into which they're now born, our narcissistic youth came jogging up behind them and as he passed, he inadvertently glanced her slender shoulder, almost toppling her and galvanising her fragile lungs. Her boyfriend shouted something and the youth briefly turned with a look of incomprehension and possibly hurt. Then as he looked in front of himself again, he saw the chance to cross the road just ahead of a stationary bus which a few elderly passengers were unhurriedly getting off. There are two lanes each way on the avenue, and he seemed unaware that a car might be passing the bus.

The sound of a thin metal shell hitting the soft tissues of the human frame is remarkably loud – horrifyingly loud – and leaves a tremor in the hands of those who hear it. Suddenly they saw the indiscernible thread that holds us up and keeps us straight. Suddenly they felt the thinness of a second that divides one reality from another. Having now heard that sound and seen the unkind trajectory of a human body catapulted into the air and falling cruelly on a hard surface designed to grip, she clung to her boyfriend's body, wanting its support but also needing to reassure herself of its physical presence, which was no less fragile than that of the poor youth out on his run. The body stirred and someone groaned. It must have been him; it contained such hurt that no one could touch or balm.

The driver got out of the van that hit the youth. He was a tall man with regular features and a sallow complexion: an Italian, a Spaniard or possibly an Arab. His expression was one of horror. He walked as we might expect someone to walk in their sleep. He was slow in his movements and uncertain what he should do, but he felt drawn towards the injured man. Someone had called an ambulance, which quickly appeared, and a crowd was formed around the scene, temporarily confining the couple to the spot where they stood when the accident occurred. Two policemen escorted the driver back to their car and checked his papers. "Shouldnae be here," one notified the other, without addressing the driver at all.

"Shouldn't be here," said a grey man in a grey suit who was standing close by. "In other words, an illegal immigrant." The driver was standing still. Stillness had finally taken hold of his life. The same second that had broken the bones of the healthy youth had also brought the driver's hectic life to an abrupt halt. Everything he'd been fearful of happening had happened, and all that was left was compassion for the man who had bounced off his vehicle and landed not twenty yards away. He was responsible. He'd come all this way and suffered so many humiliations for this. What would they do with him?

In that moment he felt the grey man's hard finger stabbing his shoulder just under his collarbone. He passively accepted the pain this produced, as though the grey man was kindly wanting to wake him from a bad dream. "You come over here and look what you do," the grey man screamed, and the crowd divided between those who were gladdened by the sight of a man being humiliated and those who were repelled. But all remained silent except the itinerant bank manager who had been pushing busily through the press of bodies until his eye fell upon this scene. Normally he was not a man to intervene in public altercations, given his long experience of adjudicating private ones, but suddenly he was gripped by a compelling certainty that here at last was a case in which all right belonged to one party and all wrong to the other. Addressing the policemen as though they were clerks at the office, he asked, "Are you detaining this man at the moment?"

"Well, yes," a policeman answered with untypical sheepishness for a policeman, impressed no doubt by the dress, carriage and presence of the man who spoke, "just while we check his documents." Many of these were foreign, and the officers of the law looked genuinely perplexed.

"Why, then, are you allowing him to be harangued by a member of the public?" the bank manager asked with crushing logic. The policemen were nettled, and now aware that they had failed in their duty in a public space. They remained silent as they mulled over the possibilities. They could have aggressively dismissed the man, but felt he was like a gambler who knows he has a good hand and is always willing to raise the stakes. The only alternative was to express some kind of humiliating apology and deal with the situation. Fortunately for them, the situation was saved by the grey man's reaction.

He left the driver and moved towards the manager with the leering fury of Sir James Goldsmith at the mention of *Private Eye*, carrying his finger before him like a weapon. He assessed the weight of the other besuited man and decided not to use it for anything but the occasional flourish in the air. "These people are flooding the country, and you're defending them."

"Flooding? This isn't Holland and Bangladesh, where they're crushed like sardines. This is Scotland, most of which is a soggy green desert – full of empty glens and treeless upland. And it's not a flood; it's a trickle. What do 'these people' do? They work far too much for far too little."

"There's nothing worse," the grey man said, "than a do-gooder in a suit."

The manager regretted entering this argument; he saw that it would be difficult to extricate himself without losing his dignity. You cannot debate with the irrational. The accountant ignored figures when it came to this subject.

But the manager realised there was no way back: "Besides, we're not talking of people, but of one human being making his difficult way through life. What just happened to him could have happened to anyone here. The runner came out into the road without looking – an act so irresponsible that he must have been distracted. Now he's paying a terrible price for that momentary lapse, but the blame cannot be placed at the door of this young man who was going about his daily business." He felt the rhetoric rising within him. He believed in what he was saying, but he believed in it more strongly now that he was saying these things so publicly. Momentarily, this was who he was: a champion of the poor and mistreated and a scourge of racists and bigots alike.

"What kind of country do we want to be? One in which the colour of your skin counts more than justice and the rule of law? How many of us saw what happened? We mustn't observe injustice and just pass by."

When he had started to speak, the party of revulsion was perhaps in the minority, but as he argued rightly but, most important, magisterially, the crowd began to shift, and as he came to the last line, it clapped its majority opinion quite clearly. The grey accountant observed in horror and slipped into the anonymity of the concourse that thinks as one and can shift in either direction. The policemen sensed that the crowd was losing interest, and waved it to disband, reassuming their professional superiority: "There's an injured man who has to be removed from the accident area. Please move on."

The bank manager felt deflated. Or rather elation and guilt cohabited his brain. He had spoken up and righted a wrong, but was there something shallow in his behaviour? He was not given to moral assertions, and he had acted on instinct. He looked towards the driver in search of a smile perhaps, or worse, an expression of gratitude. To his surprise, he saw that the man had heard nothing. He was staring at the paramedics about to lift the stretcher into the back of the ambulance, and was lost in thought. The brief scene had been nothing and the bank manager was a bit part in a modern tragedy. The driver's problems were unchanged.

The couple set off again. She was visibly shaken and said, "Nobody knows. I know better than most what'll happen to me, but nobody knows." He nodded glumly to show he understood, but had no desire to revisit that conversation.

They sat down at a table and ordered teas. In the corner of the room a tall, gangly and large-boned woman was hunched beautifully at the piano. She started to play a ripple of fast notes. The music manipulated the minds that ruminated in the crowded café, uniting them in a sensation of melancholic joy that tingles the nerves of the arms and legs, and communicating to them a sweetness that each interpreted in an entirely different manner. She finished with another flourish, rose from her chair and turned – her long, curling, black hair parting to reveal an older face than expected, a kindly one that spoke of trials and suffering overcome at great cost, but overcome nonetheless.

Three Grumpy, Half-"Celtic" Authors, a Fool and a Peer of the Realm Get Along Unswimmingly

The arty-farties, what a lot! Personally I've always kept a wide berth. And the worst of them are writers. So I have to tell you about the motley crew I met on the Isle of Archasamby last summer. A rum affair, and that's for sure.

I'm a doer, not a talker, so this does not come easy. How did it happen? Well, I went to do some shooting on the estate of our old school chum Bumper Jones. A fat kid with jug ears, extravagant freckles and an obsession with Black Sabbath. His father was a brewer. Now, I'm not the type who likes to waste his time; I like to get out there and bag them from day one. It started to rain as soon as I got there, and it was unrelenting. We did go out in the wet on the first morning, but frankly it was miserable. The following day we sat around and played Monopoly and Trivial Pursuit, while imbibing some damn good whisky or *ooshka baya* as they call it there. I always say, "Drink the local tipple and you get the right type of hangover for wherever you are." But on the third day, this became a bit of a bore. Really, what do the natives do in a place like this? No shops to speak of. No clubs. No women you'd want to sleep with or have on your arm in smart society. No smart society. No money circulating and making you and others rich. That last one of course is all the attraction. Even a City gent like me has to get away from it now and then. Recharge the old batteries.

The day after that, I had to get out of the house. Bumper, it's true, has a damn good house. A Victorian statement of power. Of course such places really need a large crew of chambermaids, preferably pretty, but Bumper doesn't make serious money and can't afford chambermaids, pretty or not. So there are just a couple of old ladies who come in three days a week for a bit of desultory dusting. Bumper asked his guests to help with the washing-up, which was a bit thick. I refused of course. "Bumper," I said, "I haven't touched a dishcloth in forty years; not since I went to stay with my demented grandmother at the age of sixteen, and I can tell you, I did not like it. I have no intention of taking up dish drying at my age."

Bumper looked offended as Bumper often does. But that just makes me go on the attack: "Bumper, another thing I've been meaning to tell you: what sort of entertainment have you put on for your guests? I've been here for three days now, and apart from the odd glass of good whisky, it has been a complete disaster. Now, what are you going to do for us?"

Bumper has always been a bit wet. Inherited the brewery business from a father who was as wet as he is. Not just wet, but boring too. Still, they are called Jones, so what can you expect? So, instead of getting angry over my outburst, he became terribly, terribly apologetic. Vomit-makingly apologetic. A regular Uriah Heep. He would see what he could do and so forth.

Back he came with two glasses of whisky and an idea, which actually turned out to be quite a good one if you are into that sociological kind of thing. Well, it was a change, and I got to see how some curious chaps like to pass their time. "Jonathan," he said, "I've thought of something to get you out of the house. I've just been on the phone to Crawford-Mackenzie." He paused as though he expected a reaction.

"The author," he said.

"Never heard of him," I clarified.

"You must have heard of Crawford-Mackenzie. The famous

writer. He wrote an autobiographical masterpiece called *The Road to Perdition*, and his *Bountiful Booze in Barra* was turned into a highly successful movie."

I hate it when people try to fill my brain with such rubbish. "Never heard of him," I insisted.

Bumper looked a little put out, and less certain of his good idea. "Well, he *is* famous, and he lives down the road. And I thought you would like to meet him."

"What are the alternatives?"

Bumper shrugged his shoulders.

"Okay then. When are we going?"

"Ah well, this is the interesting bit. It turns out that he is having a couple of writer friends over at four o'clock tomorrow afternoon, and he's got a house guest who is some kind of scribbler too, although I couldn't quite understand where he fits in."

Clearly Bumper and I have different ideas of what is interesting.

"One," he continued, "is a likeable chap who does travel books and writes funny poetry. Geoffrey Hamilton-MacNiff he's called. His *I Crossed the Channel* is an aloof and fanciful study of just how strange the French really are."

"What about the other one?" I asked hopefully.

"What other one?"

"The other writer?"

"Oh well, you won't have heard of him. No one has. A strange fellow. Bit of a leftie. Hans Bonetti-MacDonald. His *Golden Symposium* is a dialogue between Jesus Christ, Mohammed, Buddha and John Lennon."

"Bit of a rum do."

"Heap of shit actually. I only read it because he lives over on the other side of the Island. If you ask me, the fellow isn't all there, but all sorts wash up here. I don't know how the locals can put up with it."

Well the prognosis was not good. But what can a chap do? In the absence of any other entertainment and with another three days of torrential rain likely to follow, I decided to join the fun.

At four the next day we all set off. I almost changed my mind. Why, I said to myself, would I want to listen to a few arty-farties sounding off? Who knows if this Crawford-Mackenzie fellow's whisky is as good as Bumper's? But out of inertia, I let myself be drawn along. Good job too. Quite a scene it was.

I was well equipped for the weather, but Bumper, who lives on this sodden island all year round, only put an anorak over his tweed jacket, so the legs of his corduroy trousers were soaking by the time we reached the home of the writer everyone had heard of, except me. It was an agreeably plain early nineteenth-century house – a Telford manse, I was told – and it combined Presbyterian solidity with middle-class cosiness. A high wall surrounded the house, and a tall birch tree stood proudly in a corner of the front garden – an unusual sight on this treeless and windswept island.

Well, Crawford-Mackenzie's secretary met us at the door and ushered us in to a small but welcoming hall that smelt of damp wood and dusty carpet, which seemed appropriate to the spartan but comforting antiquity of a house to be visited but not lived in. We were told that Crawford-Mackenzie was only just getting up. So we sat around and she brought us some whisky. Hamilton-MacNiff was already there and complaining about how slowly people move on the Isle of Archasamby, but he didn't seem to move much himself. In fact he seemed to spend his time on absurdly long, solitary walks across deserted areas and sitting around in bars observing other people while they were pausing for a quick drink. I'm not sure how he can make a living, but clearly his parents can afford to keep him. They may not have sent him to Eton like us, but they apparently could afford some minor public school.

Crawford-Mackenzie came in wearing his dressing-gown, and he is quite a character. He belongs to another age, and only in that remote spot could such an intractably old-fashioned man of indisputable intelligence survive and even flourish. He smiled cordially at me and Hamilton-MacNiff. "Geoffrey, good to see you," he said in a deep, sonorous but rather subdued voice. To me he said nothing as, clearly in early-morning mode, he had no idea who I was, which was the first surprise of the evening.

The first conversation of note concerned the islands. Crawford-Mackenzie has strong – and somewhat barmy – opinions on this subject, and this was good because in itself the question was of no interest to me. The other writer, Hans Bonetti-MacDonald, had just come in. He, too, looked like he had swum to the house underwater with his clothes on. He had removed his boots on entering, and a blackened toe was protruding from one of his once white socks. His dark hair was turning grey, but he could not have been over forty. He sat down heavily in an armchair, as though he were in his own house, and, having caught his breath, he looked up at Crawford-Mackenzie and said, "Hi there, Charles, good to see you again."

Crawford-Mackenzie seemed genuinely pleased to see him. He said, "And it's always a pleasure to see you, Hans. Help yourself to whisky. Dorothy left the tray in the corner." What they had in common, God knows.

Hamilton-MacNiff returned to what appeared to be his favourite subject: the supposed indolence of the natives. Crawford-Mackenzie seemed angered by these speculations, but he was too much of a gentleman to deny or attack them. Instead he came up with his lunatic thesis: "But it's the place that makes them like that, damn it! It's the west wind that makes them so distinct. It bludgeons them constantly and they survive. Only the toughest can avoid being twisted and stunted by the endless power of the wind. Like the trees. Of course, it always saps your strength: that is why the Gaels are lazier than the Shetland Islanders; that is why the Gaels are more reflective and creative."

"Oh, please, do we have to talk in endless stereotypes," Bonetti-MacDonald remarked drearily, taking his first sip of whisky.

"You'd prefer to be hemmed in by every politically correct prejudice against prejudice," Crawford-Mackenzie laughed. "That is why you're so boring, Hans. Do they have a west wind in Italy?"

"Of course they have a west wind. Everyone has a west wind. In fact the Italians have special names for three winds: the north-westerly *Maestrale*, the northerly *Tramontana* which brings the cold and damp down from the mountains, and the *Scirocco* which carries the hot, dry and sometimes dusty air of the African desert."

"Small wonder the Italians are a befuddled people. Better to be battered always from the same direction."

I was delightfully confused by these people. At this stage, principally by their strange names, so I made my first foray into their madness. "Why just the Italian winds, Mr. Bonetti-MacDonald? You must be an expert in German ones too."

"My mother was half-German and half-Gael, and my father Italian. I never learnt German; nor did I ever live in Germany."

"An exotic background."

"Hardly" was his curt reply.

"How did you end up here?"

"I inherited my maternal grandmother's croft. One place is as good as another."

"I see that you like to make your own way in life," I said sarcastically.

But he replied, "I do."

Then he took a real swig of his whisky, squared towards me and smiled provocatively: "Who do you vote for?"

"Do you need to ask?" I answered a little stiffly – you know me when I pretend to be offended.

"I do. You see I'm always looking for interesting people who defy their own stereotypes."

"Sorry to disappoint you, then. I vote in accordance with what is expected of me. I vote Tory. How could I vote for anything else?"

"Well, I thought there was a good chance of your being Lib-Dem or UKIP, just for the hell of it. But surely someone like you could now go with Labour? Why not? Very reliable – for you!"

Now I was enjoying myself. The little twit was getting wound up. I stretched myself as though I were supremely comfortable, not only in Crawford-Mackenzie's baggy and badly sprung armchair but also in the whole of my worldly existence – as though I had never felt a moment of panic, pain or loss, which of course I have, and I asked expansively, "Why is it that human beings so often believe mistakenly that, whatever our political, religious and philosophical differences, we all share a common morality and thought process? That's the reason for your insane but rather touching faith in persuasion through sound reasoning. I'm not political like you people. I'm not political at all. I don't even like the Tories. They're venal and often stupid. People shouldn't vote for people because they like them."

"I can agree with that – at least in part – but why do *you* vote for them?"

"You're right, I do find Labour very reliable these days, and they should be let into government every now and then, just to stop them from feeling hurt and restless – and going off into a leftward tailspin. But how can I put it? – When the Conservative Party is in power, it is as though God is in His heaven and everything and everybody is in its proper place. And the proper place for the Tories is in government, even though most of them are jumped-up shopkeepers or old Etonians too stupid to find a proper job."

Perhaps this conversation would have wandered on. Perhaps I would have really riled them. Fate or chance had decided otherwise: we had an unexpected visitor. Lord Macmillan of Archasamby is a tall, cadaverous man. He is energetic and intelligent, and has an almost religious belief in the omniscience, perspicacity and bountifulness of a single entity: himself. In this he differs little from most politicians. And these are necessary men: someone has to take unpopular decisions and coat them with a sugar of lies. Of course this is a trade that requires lashings of self-deception. I call a spade a spade, as does Bumper in his hesitant self-deprecating way. So do these writer fellows in their absurdly tortuous, show-offy way. But a politician must call it by another name, and believe in whatever distortion circumstance demands. How that must poison their lives, poor things.

The body language was fascinating. Lord Macmillan was in a hurry and clearly wanted to speak to the master of the house – alone. I also got the impression that he did not take a liking to Hamilton-MacNiff, who he didn't know, and detested Bonetti-MacDonald, who clearly he did. When I was introduced to him, his face brightened up wonderfully, and he squeezed my hand hard with all the strength from his thin but sinewy arms. "I've always wanted to make your acquaintance, Mr. Kentley," he said.

"How do you know of my existence," I asked wearily.

"Our government was very conscious of the city's importance. I made it my business to know who the movers and shakers were."

"Call me Peregrine," I said coldly. I cannot stand New Labour politicians. They have no taste.

He of course was only too pleased to make a great display of his newly acquired status. It was to be Peregrine this and Peregrine that all evening. And he did stay once he was aware of my presence.

Bonetti-MacDonald was continuing the conversation without us, and they were still talking about these people called Gaels, who quite frankly I had never heard of. "The Gaels, like all other minority cultures in Europe, will only be Gaels for as long as they keep their language. If they lose it, they will be like everyone else – and any pretence to retain their distinctiveness will be a stupid ethnic myth. No one's ethnicity is distinct, only their culture."

"You lot are not Gaels," said Lord Macmillan dismissively, "so what can you know about it."

"We're more Gaelic than you are," the three writers replied in unison, and somehow their English, public-school accents made this statement sound ridiculous. There followed a long, heated and rather scholastic debate about what constituted a Gael and what did not. It appeared that Lord Macmillan came from the main town on the island and did not, in fact, speak Gaelic, while the three writers lost points ethnically because none of their fathers were Gaels: a Lowlander, an Englishman and, good heavens, an Italian.

"Do you mind me adding a note of reality to your discussion?" I said grandly, and you know how I enjoy lording it up, as though I cared a damn. "Surely in this globalised world in which people are migrating by the million from one continent to another, there can be little point in arguing over whether a person is wholly or one-quarter Gael. Does it really matter if this person speaks or doesn't speak a dying language? Sorry if I say things as they are, rather than as they appear to you in your febrile imaginations."

"Peregrine, you're quite right to bring them back down to earth," said Lord Macmillan, who had been denying the right of his fellow human beings to pronounce on a particular subject if they didn't come from one-hundred-per-cent island stock.

Hamilton-MacNiff was off from the blocks before his New-Labour lordship had finished talking: "You think we're guided by our imaginations? How wrong can a person be? We're guided by the overriding problems of our time – the global ones and the local ones. For centuries – millennia perhaps – we've been trashing this ball of molten rock coated with a thin layer of solid rock and earth, but only now that pollution is reaching critical levels are we giving the question any thought – and we're reacting far too slowly. Humanity has not invented a system capable of conserving our shrinking world, and probably never will. We spend billions on preserving old buildings and ancient artefacts, but when a corporation dumps toxic waste in the Ivory Coast, a judge issues a super-injunction to protect the culprit: could we get further away from a proper tutelage of the environment that sustains us?"

"Deary me!" I said, "you boys are a bundle of laughs. As though your rain hadn't depressed me enough, I now have to listen to your scare stories."

"It might help you to think," said Bonetti-MacDonald.

"To think?" I objected. "I do plenty of that. I spend almost every waking hour thinking about how to make money. That's why I'm rich and you chaps haven't got more than a few thousand pounds between you."

"To think about human existence and its betterment," Hamilton-MacNiff persevered.

"Why would I want to do that? That would be meddling. We're all here to look after number one, and if we could peer into your three brains one by one, we'd find that, behind all the rhetoric, this is exactly what each of you is after. It's just that you're not very good at it. Envy," I cried, "just envy. You'd love to be as rich as me."

"You poor unfortunate gentleman," said Crawford-Mackenzie.
"Not poor. Definitely not poor. And the happier for it."
"You must have a few hundred thousand in the bank, Charles,"
said Bonetti-MacDonald, "after the publication of *Bountiful Booze*
and *Road to Perdition*."
"Never counted," said Crawford-Mackenzie snootily, "one
should never count one's money. Money looks after itself, in my
opinion."
"My God," I said, "you really are from another time. Money
doesn't look after itself. Never did. Certainly doesn't now. I considered you a fellow Tory."
"I am," Crawford-Mackenzie said. "Don't you know that the
most bitter and significant differences are to be found within par-
ties and not between them?"
"I'm not that interested in politics, to tell you the truth," and I
wasn't lying, although I did find their politics fascinating in their
absurdity.
Hamilton-MacNiff could not sit still in his chair, and he leaned
across to me in his enthusiasm, "Charles is a very special kind
of Tory in this Tory-free nation: he is a Romantic Jacobite, more
interested in the politics of two and three hundred years ago,
than growth figures and the performance of the stock exchange.
Idealising the past isn't that different from idealising the future. I
like to think of him as one of us; nothing to do with you people
at all."
"I think your judgement," I said, "is clouded by friendship and
friendly rivalry. It is not the product of clear analysis, something
you writer fellows aren't that good at. I have no idea what a
Romantic Jacobite might be, and have no desire to be enlightened
on the subject. Scottish politics were always more Byzantine than
most, and life is a short affair." A statement, I have to admit, that
was based on absolutely no knowledge of their politics now or at
any other time. It's amazing how a certain delivery and self-belief
can give an impression of expertise and even wisdom.
I could feel them bristle. It was such fun. Almost as good as
being up a hill and blasting off at the fauna. Unfortunately the

peer of the realm thought that he had to come to my rescue: "The universe of the ideal and the imagination might have its place in the arts, but for practical men like Peregrine and myself it is only a diversion."

I think that I was perhaps part of the absurdity of the situation, and not just an onlooker. Lord Macmillan wanted to talk the kind of voodoo economics that drives me up the wall. There is no one more Thatcherite than a New-Labour politician, and when they become lords, they no longer have to pay lip service to left-wing politics. They pursue the board room more determinedly than anyone else and their belief in free markets has no bounds. The fact is, all that political economics – macroeconomics as Lord Macmillan of Archasamby no doubt calls it – is of no interest. The far from predictable business of knowing how to make money in the banking system is enough for me and, while I'm hugely thankful to Thatcher for sorting out the unions and making it possible for me to become much richer than I otherwise would have, I can't say that I ever liked the grocer's daughter or her absurd Churchillian pretensions. But every now and then, you need a politician like her and, for a generation or two, you're fine. The proof is precisely in all these Labour politicians who practically stalk you. In their youth, they wouldn't have given a chap like me the time of day, and now they want to hang on my every word. Of course, you have to humour them: invite them to dinners, flatter them, wrap up your ideas in their repulsive, nonsensical politically-correct jargon, and that sort of thing. Small price to pay, but it is a bit nauseating when one pops up while you're trying to have a quiet and diverting holiday in one of the most rain-soaked parts of the world. Well, it had seemed like a good idea.

"You two talk as though the credit crunch never happened" were the words Hamilton-MacNiff used to interrupt me, and I was very glad of his overdue interruption.

"Shop talk is always dull," I said with urbane civility. "And how rude of me, particularly in the light of our host's excellent whisky and the scintillating conversation." Not scintillating enough to prevent Bumper from falling asleep near the fire. "Do you think the credit crunch to be a game-changer then?"

"Certainly," said Hamilton-MacNiff, "you'd have to be an idiot to think otherwise."

"Would you?" I feigned interest and surprise, and then added in a different key, "Do you take time out from writing novels and poetry to reflect deeply on the economic crisis? Can you think of a way out of it?"

My sarcasm went down badly. They like to fight amongst themselves, these writer fellows, but they stand together against the outsider. "There isn't a solution," he returned, "capitalism is inherently dysfunctional. The only solution is to change society."

"Do you agree with this?" I asked Crawford-Mackenzie. "Surely not."

"I agree that this society is not sustainable, but I feel we need to move back to a time of hard work and sound values."

"Here we go," Bonetti-MacDonald finally joined the fray. "What would those times think of people who get up at four in the afternoon and start on their first whisky immediately after their toast and tea?"

"Writers are always an exception," Crawford-Mackenzie produced a beguiling smile that was both smug and complicit.

"Sounds elitist to me," said Hamilton-MacNiff.

"I am an elitist," Crawford-Mackenzie laughed, and I had to agree with him.

"Our society," I said, "has produced unprecedented levels of liberty and affluence. So what do you people want to put in its place?"

"Paternalism," said Crawford-Mackenzie. "A free market, yes. Or at least freeish. But a responsible society in which those who know best can work freely in the interests of the whole."

"And how would this work?" I asked. "I hate to spoil the party, but isn't this pie in the sky. That society is gone forever." Lord Macmillan of Archasamby snorted with laughter.

"I'm not a constitutionalist," Crawford-Mackenzie said defiantly and quite reasonably. "We need to create a society that knows where it is going – and not too far. How we do it is not something I feel obliged to answer."

"How very convenient," I said, also quite reasonably. "Have we any other offers at this sale of the utopias?"

"A return to the post-war consensus," Hamilton-MacNiff showed his colours. "A return to Keynesianism and full employment. A return to high growth, the welfare state and good universal and free education."

"Ah, so one wants to return to the distant past and the other to the recent past," I was getting into my stride, as though I had just caught sight of a stag on the brow of the hill – a perfect shot, as long as I make the approach carefully and quietly. "I thought that writers were supposed to use their imagination."

"Communism," said that wilful Hans Bonetti-MacDonald.

"Communism?" I pretended to be shocked, but my heart leapt with joy. This was one I would enjoy tearing apart. "Doesn't that also belong to a recent past that feels more ancient than Crawford-Mackenzie's Romantic whatever-its-called?"

They laughed, I'll give them that. Even Bonetti-MacDonald, clearly the radical of this crew.

"Of course, the fall of the Soviet Union was your great victory," he said, "and the West even found a way to make money from it, although the human cost turned out to be high for the ex-Soviet citizens. But communism will always be one of the options. I don't say that it will prevail. There has been too much soothsaying, but the idea cannot be eradicated. In fact, defeat can lead to victories. Have you never heard of Pyrrhus of Epirus?"

Actually I have little time for people who say, "Have you never head of ...?" – particularly if they end the question with the name of a Greek general or Greek anybody, for that matter. I had vaguely heard of a "pyrrhic victory", so I said, "Of course, the Battle of Epirus." And they laughed knowingly. Well, they have little else to do in their lives but collect pointless factoids. I had clearly failed to wing it, and I wasn't going to pursue the matter. "I'm surprised that you can defend a state that had such a terrible human rights record."

"It was never about human rights," Bonetti-MacDonald got on a high horse he was clearly well acquainted with. "America trumpeted the Helsinki Agreement, even as it brought back the chain gang. Now that the Soviet Union no longer exists, it's time to admit that in some areas it was spectacularly successful. I do not speak of its grotesque crimes against humanity – principally its own citizens and indeed its most fervent supporters – because that should be obvious. There were other lesser evils in the Soviet Union, which arrived there earlier and have become increasingly familiar aspects of modernity everywhere."

"I thought you were a communist," I was getting a little confused.

"I am. Productive capital and, in particular, land should belong to the commonality. Those evils arrived in the Soviet Union not because it was communist, but because it was, briefly, the most modern society there was, even as it struggled to feed its people under the blows of three dozen foreign invasions. Perhaps these evils of modernity can never be reversed. Perhaps we should learn to live with them, but why should we pretend that they don't exist?"

"How preposterous!" I shouted, practically unable to process the absurdity of his arguments. "What possible connection could there be between our current democracies and the murderous and unnatural regime that called itself the Soviet Union? The self-proclaimed socialist state, but really a malign and shambolic parody of a Western empire."

"Of course there were disagreeable aspects about the Soviet life, and under Stalin's criminal regime there was worse, but many of those disagreeable aspects were innovations that have been transferred to our capitalist societies in quite recent times. Advanced techniques of mass advertising were first developed in Russia in the twenties. Gorky's obsession with the plain language of working people is everywhere in our press, TV and now almost every other media. The Soviets invented rule by the focus group, by testing ideas on samples of workers and peasants. The idea stinks, because the minute you form such a group, they cease to be typical. Besides this is not rule by the majority, but rule by the uninformed, by those who do not care, by those who reply on a coerced impulse to a question they very probably have never posed themselves."

"Is that it?" I sighed with unalloyed boredom.

"No, there's more. There's the rule of a semi-educated and bullying bureaucratic class that armed with some branch of pseudo-science or real science misapplied pokes its judge-mental nose everywhere. To challenge their current truths is defined as madness or at least as childish obtuseness. There's near total conformism in the media. Now that CCTV and Google drones can observe us everywhere, there's a level of surveillance that never existed in the Soviet Union, but only in that great caricature of it, *1984*. Was Orwell satirising Soviet communism or modernity as it would evolve? The capital-ist state is everywhere, but worse, it often acts with impunity through a privatised agency."

"Our societies may not be perfect," I admitted, "but our people can think what they want and do what they want."

"Can they?" continued Bonetti-MacDonald, "Can they now? Civilians are always compromised with the regime under which they eat and sleep. They commit small acts of evil in the pur-suit of petty interests, whilst armies commit great evils often in the name of great ideals. Soldiers make sacrifices in an artificial morality where aims are pure, whereas civilians act heroically in the real world of lesser evils. That is why we should be fearful of all militaristic language – it is the language of over-simplification. But the Soviet Union had settled down, and was trying to create a civil society within socialism; what right had we to step in and subvert it?"

The man was deranged, but I continued to engage: "The prob-lem was equality itself. Stalin was an egalitarian, was he not?"

"So you think it takes an egalitarian to introduce equality. What a strange idea! To change the world either for the better or for the worse, you need men of conviction who will do anything – anything, I tell you – to make their certainties real. The trick is to get rid of them once the change is complete, as the Athenians did with Themistocles, who helped consolidate democracy and fought off the Persians. And the interesting question is: does the idea make the man or the man the idea? Geoffrey, with his love of dialectic, will say it is a bit of both, but I know that the idea moulds the man, and does so roughly, as a clumsy child moulds a piece of clay. The man, however powerful he is, is a plaything of the idea, and he ends up doing unimaginable things, by which I mean things *he* could not have imagined. His dreams become a nightmare, and caricatures of themselves – but still they inspire. Hope and despair go hand in hand, and lead us towards their uncertain future."

"Enough of politics," said his lordship, whose expression had become increasingly concerned as the conversation developed – concerned in the manner of the modern politician, with his head tilted slightly to one side, indicating empathy no doubt. His facial expression skilfully and indeed unbelievably combined indulgence and moral outrage. "I'm sure that Peregrine didn't come all this way to get a political lecture on the wonders of the Soviet Union. I would have thought that we moved on from that long ago. You're all writers and I think that's why Peregrine came to see you." He turned to me to digress politely, "Shame about the weather. I hope you weren't too disappointed."

"Actually," I uttered with theatrical moroseness, "I would have preferred to be visited by three or four footballers, actresses, beauty queens or TV cooks. Having said that, the conversation has been unexpectedly entertaining if somewhat bizarre, and the whisky has been unreservedly good. My advice to you all, though, is that you should never travel too far from your straitjackets."

Crawford-Mackenzie chortled, Hamilton-MacNiff was insulted and Bonetti-MacDonald laconically delivered that old cliché: "It takes one to know one."

His lordship, clearly unused to conversation that didn't fit a template, was so much at a loss that he just ignored what I had said and continued to announce his arbitration: "Given that he came to see writers, I suggest that you discuss writing."

"Start there, and it could go anywhere," said the ever loquacious Bonetti-MacDonald. "I thought I was coming round for a few drinks. Turns out I have to earn them like a performing seal." He flapped his arms at his side and made a noise vaguely reminiscent of a seal's bark. He was the only one who found this amusing.

Hamilton-MacNiff, the class swat, took up the challenge, but did not raise his arm and I'm not sure teacher would have liked his turn of phrase: "The novel is fucked. It has run out of things to say."

"Not at all," said Bonetti-MacDonald. "It's going through a bad patch, and will return as strong as ever. This has happened in the past."

Hamilton-MacNiff, intelligent and aloof, sneered and said, "The world changes but Hans will always live in the nineteen-sixties, the decade before he was born. If only that were the case. The corporations that now monopolise the book industry and the demise of the Net Book Agreement mean that the blockbuster will take over, genre will reign and innovation will end."

"Rubbish," said Crawford-Mackenzie, waking from a reverie, "who cares about the Net Book Agreement. Leave that stuff to the accountants. The world changes much less than you think and you shouldn't get too obsessed about the technology that appears to dominate our lives. Of course, it changes things – mainly for the worse – but ultimately we all have to sleep, eat, work, make love, possibly reproduce, grow old, fail and die. That always accounted for ninety per cent of what it meant to be a human and it still does. You both accuse me of believing in a golden age, and perhaps there was for humanity, but the novel is a different thing. The novel thrives on misery and exploitation. How else did Tsarist Russia produce such fine literature? And how else did the most terrible years of Stalin's repression produce the same result? The novel has work to do at the moment, and when that's the case, it will always find a way to renew itself."

"I agree with both of you – to some extent," said Bonetti-MacDonald. "Yes, there is more continuity than we currently think, because we're dazzled by the strangeness of technological change. It is also true that the novel thrives in some conditions and not in others. Our times are not good for the novel, but I don't think the problems are primarily about the book market."

"What are they then?" said Hamilton-MacNiff, so wearied he seemed to have trouble in articulating his jaw. Perhaps this is an argument they revisit often – when in their cups.

"The humanistic discourse I associate with the novel has perhaps run its course," said Bonetti-MacDonald. "As a teenager I was politicised by a passage in Tolstoy's *Resurrection*, which concerned an aristocratic child's inability to empathise with the poor who surround him in nineteenth-century Moscow. There's a book by Ian McEwan which attempts to do the exact opposite: the central character – perhaps representing the author's views – muses about the tramp who disfigures the square below his house. He feels sorry for the penniless man in a perfunctory manner, but goes on to say that this is an inevitable state of affairs: in the jungle of life, there must be losers. Presumably McEwan has earned his right to pass on his genes through the brilliance of his novels – but what if he had been born before the invention of writing or printing or the novel itself; what if he were to be born in a hundred years when, according to Geoffrey, the novel will be dead – the fact that they've been announcing the death of the novel for decades does not mean that it won't die one day; what if he were born in times when it's impossible to collect royalties and everything is pirated?"

"Of course," said Hamilton-MacNiff, "you can't use literary talent to validate Darwinism. The trouble with isms is that you're expected to reject them or swallow them whole: of course there's evolution; that has been proven beyond all doubt. It may well be that survival of the fittest is one of the most important drivers for evolution, but it cannot be applied to everything in the natural world, and certainly not to human society as it is currently organised – for a period of time that can have had no effect on our genetic make-up. Darwinism applied to modern capitalist society is the new eugenics."

"Yes, yes," replied Bonetti-MacDonald, "that may well be. I'm not interested in all that macro stuff. Leave that to the scientists and other bores. The novelist must be a humanist: he has to be on the side of that tramp, he has to understand how that condition could happen to any one of us."

"I doubt it," I said, but they ignored me as they got angrier with each other.

"The poet," said Bonetti-MacDonald, "dresses up the banal in fine clothing. This is not a criticism of poetry, which is much more artistic than the novel. So the prose-writer has to make up for being prosaic by being more profound. He has to dig around ceaselessly to find an idea that's original, which today means the idea behind an idea behind another idea. The novelist has to start with the tramp, who is a tragic figure condemned to an early death amongst great wealth – while hypothermia drains his potentially healthy body, the guys with the healthy genes, or is it bank balances, are kept alive even into extreme dotage when perhaps they'd prefer to die if only they'd retained the powers of speech to communicate that preference."

"You can't say that the novel is anything," said Crawford-Mackenzie, "it's not inherently humanist and it's not inherently anti-humanist. It can be anything. Its only limitation is that it can't be wholly anything; there has to be a conflict."

I had been half aware of the presence of a strange individual: scrawny to the point of anorexia, he seemed slightly uncontrolled in his movements. Occasionally he would grin, as if in relation to some internal dialogue. It had been impossible to know whether or not he was following the conversation until he suddenly intervened in a tremulous, slightly high-pitched voice – not without a certain authority – that came from God knows where. Perhaps from a peculiar form of detachment, which emerged as the evening progressed. "These writers are too tall to see what's going on, too relaxed to feel how life can sting and to clever to write a fool's part."

I must have looked a little surprised.

"Have you not been introduced to the fool?" asked Bonetti-MacDonald.

"No," I answered, "isn't that title a little cruel, however much it might appear to accurately reflect reality?"

"He was the one who claimed the title as his own," Bonetti-MacDonald explained. "He boasts that he is both a fool and a coward, but I'm not convinced that he's any more foolish or cowardly than the rest of us."

"Clever," I said and translated the concept into business-speak, "what they call 'negative sell'."

"Not at all," the fool objected, "I'm not guilty of affectation – possibly the most corrosive force in society because it's so widespread. It may be that I haven't yet achieved a state of total folly and cowardice, but this achievement is not a boast but an ambition."

"He's the author of several books," Bonetti-MacDonald continued to speak up for him.

"All of them unpublished," the fool said proudly, renewing his inane grin.

"So you too have a passion for writing," I said condescendingly, realising that the fool enjoyed a degree of respect in this company.

"Why not?" he said. "Any fool can write."

"You think the other writers are too political?" I asked him.

"Not at all. I think they are too theoretical – too settled in their beliefs."

"But can you go on forever not knowing and never reaching a conclusion?"

"Well, yes and no. You have a point. Although a writer should not conclude, he should invent a new way of not understanding in each of his books. We write to push things away. Folly is also a state of restlessness."

The conversation with him was most amusing thing so far. I wanted to encourage him, but had little grasp of the subject. "Are you part of a school or do you want to found one?"

The fool laughed his unsettling laugh as if I had intended to joke and he were lauding the subtlety of my witticism. "You clearly know the answer," he said irritatingly. "Post-modern novelists treat the novel as though they had invented it. Cleverness is fine. There is a place for cleverness, but without folly it is worthless."

"What does that mean?"

He looked at me with surprise.

"Simple," he said, "if you write a novel to examine the human condition, you have to be in the novel and suffer with it. If you write a novel to examine the novel, you have to be outside it and unfeeling. By making what I said this explicit I am almost guilty of what I'm criticising: the obsession with form within a form."

"You seem pretty obsessed with form yourself," I observed.

"You have a point. We become what we criticise, and what we praise eludes us."

"You guys make my head spin," I said with a degree of duplicity. I was enjoying myself and wanted to flatter them. "I can't wait to get back to the office and relax my brain a while."

"You think we're bad? You should try the poets," said Hamilton-MacNiff. "Complete loonies."

The whisky was beginning to have its effect on my mind, and I was careless of my company. "Poetry, never had much time for it, but as we're in male company let me recite my favourites: 'A woman is only a woman, but a good cigar is a smoke.' Anyone want a cigar, by the way?" I extracted my cigar box from my jacket pocket. "Only the best." They looked at me with disgust, I suppose. Why they take these things so seriously, I have no idea. I hadn't quite exhausted my stock of the *Barrack-Room Ballads*: "'For the Colonel's lady and Judy O'Grady are sisters under their skins.' I'm just trying to lighten up the conversation," I pleaded against their increasing anger.

The fool jumped up shaking with fury; he pointed his finger at me and screamed over-dramatically, "You're an arse!"

"Why?" I asked quietly, with a hint of menace. Never had this happened to me before. It took a fool to present me with this ... truth? No, but an interpretation clearly shared by others. I noticed that Bumper Jones was enjoying the scene, and I remembered for the first time during my stay that he had never invited me; I had invited myself. Only Lord Macmillan defended me, but he did so mutedly: "Steady on," he muttered – an expression he must have picked up in the Upper House.

"Because your purest excretions come out of your anus. Your mouth, for instance, produces the foulest faeces ever expelled from human orifice."

"Hold on," I stood up, the alcohol was firing up my anger.

He stood his ground, but free of menace. There was no cruelty in his eyes, just outrage. The beast within me saw the weakness and reacted quickly: my fist was lifted and about to begin its trajectory towards his chin when a strong hand grabbed my wrist. I turned and saw it was Charles Crawford-Mackenzie, the famous author I'd never heard of. He had a surprisingly vice-like grip, and said coldly and succinctly, "Do not hit my guest!" I relaxed my own arm, and felt something akin to shame.

Now it was the fool who stepped forward: so close I could feel his breath on my face and could only just focus his smile, the one that is halfway between inane jocularity and insanity.

"Are you a king?" he asked, the warmth of his breath slightly perfumed with whisky.

"A king?"

"Well, I have this coin, a pound coin," he held it up. "This woman's head appears to be that of a queen, as she wears a crown – of wealth and not of thorns. Now, you are wedded to the coin, I think, so you must be a king."

"There is some logic in his thought," said Bumper Jones, "he starts from a false premise and ends up with a distorted truth."

I felt the alcohol drain from my mind, and another emotion I rarely feel assailed me, that strange and eventful evening: I felt alone and out of my own tribe; I felt that my views had no allies. I was the alien amongst that alien people.

"But what does the coin mean?" I asked, never one to give in quietly.

"It means so many things, and how we love things that mean many things."

"And what are they?"

"Do you really want to know?"

"Why not? I've heard plenty of twaddle today. A little more won't do any harm."

"Well, first of all it represents itself: money as a form of exchange. That's banal, but not unimportant."

"Okay, let's move on to the more interesting stuff."

"It represents the inability of the creative mind to be itself in this society."

"That figures. But why should the creative mind – by which I suppose you to mean arty-farty self-expression – be exonerated from the rigours of the market? If no one wants your stupid books, why should anyone publish them?"

"I haven't been published, remember, and I have no desire to be published..."

"That's your first lie!" I cried exultantly.

"Well done," said the fool with a grin, "you're a bit of a fool yourself. Who would have thought it? I should have said that I don't have desire enough to be published. You see these three published authors: only one of them ever made any money for himself and his publisher, but all three practise a degree of self-censorship to please their public or their public as the publisher perceives it."

The other three writers looked uncomfortable with the new direction of this conversation, which was quietly releasing me from the corner I'd got caught in. Of course, Crawford-Mackenzie was the least bothered, partly because he does make money and partly because he takes himself less seriously.

"Don't think," the fool was becoming too tiresome for a fool, "that I write obscurely: I write to pursue the only truth a fiction writer can attain, a truth that fits into a square inch," and he held up his pound coin, "anything bigger than that simply falls apart. We leave the explanation of the universe to non-fiction writers."

"All well and good," I said, now feeling my way back to control of the situation, "but this is just for you guys. It's of no interest to the rest of us."

"Not at all," he said mildly, "I was speaking not only of writing, but of all creative activity. And everyone has a creative mind, so it concerns all humanity."

"I think humanity wants to eat first. What else does your coin represent?"

"The commodification of everything, including those mainstays of human existence: love and friendship. It means the death of conversation and the birth of networking."

I didn't pursue that one. Surely no relationship can be entirely free of each participant's self-interest. Where would the fun be? These people don't see the beauty of market and its ability to rule our lives dispassionately. "And ..." I asked.

"The fascination it exercises beyond our wants. If you let this coin lead you on, your desire for it will outstrip your wants. You will want more financial wealth than could be justified by all your real and imagined wants in a very long life time multiplied by misery you inflicted on yourself and others to acquire it. Still more strangely, your desire for wealth will banish your other desires that were the original cause of your desire for wealth."

"Peregrine, what do you think of our island?" asked Lord Archasamby, who had had enough.

"It's wet," I said.

"But the storm's over," said the fool, who promptly stood up and left the room without further comment.

"I was thinking more in terms of your view of our culture, language and landscape. How long have you been here?" his lordship simpered.

"A few days. And I've formed no opinion at all of your island. I didn't come here on an anthropological field trip – but for some rest and entertainment."

"We still have a community here," said Hamilton-MacNiff.

"When people talk about community," said Bonetti-MacDonald, "they mean a local hierarchy – to which they very probably belong."

I had no desire to follow more of their sophistries; I preferred the incomprehensible fool. "Bumper, where's the fool gone?" I asked, now wholly relaxed with the epithet. Bumper nodded to me and took me out into the hall.

"Are you missing the fool already?" he smiled.

"He's entertaining in his own way," I said.

We climbed the stairs that spoke of both frugality and relative wealth. The occasional stair creaked appropriately and the walls displayed original paintings of Highland scenes devoid of any human presence. A small window revealed the view from the back of the house: a hill that stubbornly bore up its load of sodden peat bog topped with heather and the dark green of their wild grasses and rushes. The storm had broken and a bright but feeble sun shone on the dampness of the rock and sloping ground. Does it take courage to live here? The land itself appears to express defiance.

Bumper pointed to a door at the front of the house, and as I opened it, he went back downstairs without another word. Even when the door was fully open and I could see him busy scribbling at a desk, the fool made no attempt to acknowledge my presence. Bizarrely I felt a little diminished and unable to go forward, I coughed to draw his attention.

"You can come in, if you must," he said, still refusing to turn his head in my direction.

I came up to the desk and took out a wad of notes – amounting, I would say, to about two thousand pounds – which I placed on the desk. He continued to write. I pushed the pile of money in his direction until it was almost under his nose, which quivered as though it had detected a bad smell. He stopped writing and still did not turn in my direction. He was motionless and the hand holding the pen was frozen in the air, the absurd pretension of a mind entirely alien to my own. I got the message and gave in first by removing the money and replacing it in my jacket pocket. Only then did he turn to me and say, "I knew that you would try that on." He smiled and put his pen down. "What can I do for you?"

"Just came for a chat. What are you writing?" I asked and he removed his arms from the desk and sat back in his chair to allow me to read:

What are we fighting this war for? – asked Abram Davidovich – Russia, so vast and empty, cannot win against those little countries, dense with worn and emptied souls, and the clatter of harsh, unthinking machinery snorting steam like metallic monsters tamed by self-important men who bustle far off in luxurious offices and courtly edifices of surplus wealth purloined.

"Heavy stuff. Not the kind of thing you take down to the beach then?" I laughed.

"I rarely go to the beach," he said. Was this the literalism of the zany or just a desire not to engage?

"And what is this obsession with Russia?" I asked.

"I admire Russia because Russia admires literature. I like the fact that there literature matters because it's about what matters. It's not entertainment, but an integral part of life."

"I doubt it. You're sure that videos, satellite TV and internet porn aren't a more integral part of their lives now?"

"I've heard that they still read a lot. But it's difficult to know what's happening in Russia outside Moscow and St Petersburg – the green zones of Western affluence. Who knows what benefits of modernisation have been brought to Russia, along with MacDonalds, unemployment and child prostitution?"

"What are you actually writing about?"

"Human tragedy. The heroism of mortals. The complexity of moral decisions."

"How dull. Any sex?"

"None."

"Isn't it a little grandiloquent?"

"You're right. That's why it doesn't work in context. This character would have thought like this, but this is not the way he would have expressed himself. To write is to delete, to stop short and to avoid."

"But you always find room for your favourite theme. Money is bad, and greed the only evil."

"Of course greed is not the only evil. If a man wears his love of man like a badge of honour and uses it as an excuse to wag his finger at others, then it is merely a vanity, another form of self-love. There are many paths to egotism. Even the ascetic who lives a seemingly selfless life is vain, if looking in the mirror he smiles and says, 'I am a good man.'"

"So you agree with me in condemning all this do-gooder non-sense," I asserted, led on by the fool's erratic mind.

"No, not at all. To struggle feebly against the forces of evil and to feel the tragic sadness of this earth are the primary purposes of this life. Everyone does these things to some extent. It's beyond the powers of a poor fool to assay the purity of other people's emotions. Only God knows that…"

"If God exists."

"…if God exists. We cannot know if God is there to know, but we are born or brought up to want that final judge or justice. Even if there is no God, is it not divine, or does it not at least make us intoxicatingly alive, to struggle free of necessity?

"Animals are governed wholly by necessity," the fool continued, "and free will draws humanity towards God, because only through free will can humanity enter a moral universe – a new and separate existence. But the eternal gods cannot have morality either, because morality – quite strangely – is also created out of the contingency of necessity. In other words, absolute free will is as inimical to morality as is necessity, and morality can only exist where there is a mixture of these two opposites. If God exists, then He is a combination of free will and the tragic contingency of this world.

"Not only disease, diet, DNA, environment and chance govern and constrict us, but also the ideology we live within: consumerist capitalism drives us back down towards the animals and we elect to be no more than our mere wants. Earlier capitalism secularised morality, but in many ways made the moral choices starker and more complex."

I pulled up a chair, sat down and looked at the man: "You're a queer fish," I said, "and I won't argue with you, because I hardly understood a word you said. This much I did get: you reject material wealth. Perhaps it isn't envy, I'll grant you that. But do you look in the mirror and say 'I am a good man'?"

"Then I would really be a fool in every sense," he laughed. "I live the way I do because it makes me happy. No more, no less."

I always say, "Distrust a man who says he's happy." I say this with good reason: it is a claim I often make myself, and I know myself not to be trustworthy. But I did not say this; perhaps I should have. Instead I wanted to lower the tone of our conversation, but that isn't easy with the fool. "So what will you write about next?" I asked.

"Death," he said, and I should have guessed. "Writing these stories has made me think about death. It starts to occur long before the heart stops. My feelings are more leaden, and my energy is low."

"Was it ever high?" I asked.

He smiled: "Even lower."

"A slow death then," I exchanged his smile.

"Yes, maybe the slowness of my death will cure me of my folly. Maybe there's a post-modern writer in me yet – who will rise up sullenly from the moulted skin of joyous folly to give vent to atrophied emotions."

The fool is the most harmless of these four writers, as you've probably guessed. But he's also deceivingly entertaining, and I cannot trust him because I cannot understand him in any way.

"Why do you write then?" I asked, "to predict the future or to examine the present?" This was the moment when I decided that I really had to tell you about this lot.

Like putting a coin in a vending machine, asking the fool a question results in him spitting out your chosen flavour. "The future? Don't ask me. It is surprising how many cannot see what's happening in the present. The future is and always will be utterly beyond our comprehension, although we must always plan for it if we are to live decently in the present.

"Those who do not listen to the rumble of the distant future, but play with the received truths and prejudices of their own times should at least be aware of the immediate future, if they are to succeed: they're like the young men at the Pamplona bull run – they wait until the last possible moment to shelter from the new oncoming wisdom that will demand a new conformism. This activity requires skill, good reflexes and bravado, but personally I can never see the point of it."

"So you write to change the present," I sneered, always uncertain of what I thought of that elusive fellow.

"Nothing so grand. To mutter in the wind. To subvert it perhaps. But only by questioning and pointing to the many gaps in our knowledge. A literary work should produce a plurality of interpretations – and a compromise between the reader's mind and the author's. If there is to be a struggle for progress, it will be through information. Great minefields of lies will have to be cleared, and many will succumb to the cruel lacerations of black propaganda. In this literature will play an auxiliary role in a wider struggle of whistleblowers and leakers against power, which is ruthless and shameless. I am not optimistic, and if there's to be no progress, it's better for the individual to withdraw from society and think."

"You're remarkably frank with the enemy for someone who takes his role so seriously."

"Is it taking oneself too seriously to demand the right to mutter in the wind?"

"Well, put it another way: you have been generous to discuss your ideas with someone who clearly doesn't share them."

"To people like Charles Crawford-Mackenzie and myself, it's much more fun to chat with people we disagree with. Charles and I agree on very little, except the utility of disagreeing."

"What do you think of that Eyetie?" I asked, suggesting complicity and pressing for a division.

The fool looked at me sharply, and I immediately realised he was not fool enough not to know I was winding him up. "Bonetti-MacDonald has interesting things to say. None of those three downstairs are interested in provoking the bull of oncoming fashion. They're more interesting in pricking the elephant of power and then doing a runner. Sadly the elephant doesn't even notice, being fully aware that rational argument barely affects the manner in which humans consort with each other. All three of them believe too much in improving society and too little in the chaos and madness of mankind. This is the charming disease of rationalism."

Exasperated, I said, "At least they believe in something they can communicate. You never have the courage to take a stand on anything. This conversation would have been more useful if you had explained what you actually want and how to get it."

"You don't come to a fool for answers, only for questions."

"And I don't believe you're such a fool, either."

"What is a fool if not someone who doesn't understand anything, and I don't understand anything. Ergo, I am a fool."

I shook the fool's hand warmly – God knows why – and went downstairs in search of Bumper. He was already in the hall, and getting ready to go. I togged up as well and asked where the others were.

"In the garden. Big event. That fine-looking tree in the corner came down in the storm." We went out into the garden and two men in blue overalls – neighbours we were told – were busying around, one with a chainsaw and the other putting the cut wood into a neat pile. Hamilton-MacNiff was helping out in his usual desultory manner and Bonetti-MacDonald was inspecting the shape of the tree rings in each cross-section, as though it were a question of great moment. Our host was joking in Gaelic with the man wielding the saw, who could probably have done without the interruptions. They had started in the middle of the tree to open up the pathway it fell across, and it was now clear for us to go. Everyone was engaged with the tree incident – for them it was like a 100-point fall on the FTSE-100. We waved to them by way of a peremptory leave-taking. As we left the garden, I heard Crawford-Mackenzie say in a low but clear voice, "Who was that creep? Yes, I know he's a friend of Jones's, but what does he do? Used-car salesman?"

I heard laughter and Geoffrey Hamilton-MacNiff said in a louder voice, "Come off it, Charles, you know that's not the case. Big bucks there."

But I cannot say that I dislike them. Actually Crawford-Mackenzie was a pleasant enough chap, and this made me think about the circular nature of the likes and dislikes in that room. Writers admire politicians and seek out their company in the hope that they can influence them with their crackpot ideas, while politicians find them absurd, rootless non-entities. Yet politicians like Lord Archasamby love bankers because they went into politics to exert power, and discover that the real power is held by people like me. We bankers, however, find politicians venal, and although, as men of the world, venality does not shock us, there is nothing more pathetic than the venality of jumped-up moralisers who are always looking over their shoulders at some ill-defined public opinion. Yet in our hearts we also know that our power, which undoubtedly brings us great wealth and security, does not give us real control over events or even understanding of them. We're attracted to writers because part of us envies the freedom of their world of ideas, however ineffectual, self-deluding and often escapist it may be. They of course dismiss us, because our kind of power is not power they desire, comprehend or even find intellectually interesting. I am not talking just about ridiculous people like the enjoyably obnoxious Bonetti-MacDonald, I also mean upright and pleasantly eccentric writers like Crawford-Mackenzie, in particular, although Hamilton-MacNiff seemed a good sort, in spite of his leftie tendencies. Not, of course, that I will ever have time to read any of them.

There is something professional about Lord Archasamby, but that is deceiving. There is a hardness in him, the hardness of a businessman or financier like myself, but I don't adopt an air of moral superiority. If you pursue an amoral existence, you should be honest enough to put aside all moral codes. My amorality, or some may call it immorality, is quite sincere, just like these writer fellows. Their ideas are not real, but their sincerity cannot be doubted.

They're a curious type of fauna, and like any species in danger of extinction they provoke a nostalgic regret that approximates to compassion, but isn't. It is too weak to provoke any kind of action or reaction. When the last of them dies, it will mark the end of a pointless rebellion that cost too many lives. I like these ones because they amuse me, but if they were flourishing, I would be the first to insist on their extirpation, whatever the human, ecological or financial cost. In the sixties, seventies and even eighties, we had them bombed, napalmed, shot, thrown from planes and killed individually and anonymously in the night. Nothing to be proud of, but it had to be done. We won, and I cannot see us ever being challenged again. We can pursue our own business, which is what we were put into this world to do. The silly leftist ideology never took account of human nature.

Out on the road I saw for the first time the view down to the sea: an expanse of white sand, whose magnitude defied reality, stretched out to a shore of bright turquoise, where the shallows reflected the whiteness of that sand and mixed it with the pure blue we could see further out to sea. Visibility was as heightened as previously it had been diminished: the extremes between the different ways the same landscape dressed itself seemed almost supernatural.

"Nature," I exclaimed. "Nature trumps it all, including itself: the tree, the view and sudden change of weather. Where is man in all this? Like a limpet clinging to the rock."

"You don't say," said Bumper with distaste. "You came all the way from London to tell me that?"

"That's the point. In the city you can forget about nature, even as you walk through a leafy park. That's subservient nature; this is nature triumphant."

"Well then, you've learnt something on your trip north."

"I have, Bumper, I really have, and not just that. I've learnt that not all the world thinks like me, and I've learnt that I'll be damn glad to be back home, amongst my own hubbub, my own certainties, my own tribe – my own delusions. It has been much more fun than I would have thought, Bumper, but I won't be back."

"Very sensible. It's good to be reminded of who you are not, but only occasionally – otherwise it becomes unsettling."